**W9-BRN-591**

"For readers who miss the kind of fast-paced, idea-rich science fiction that Heinlein, Asimov, and Clarke produced at the height of their powers, this is just the ticket."

—*San Francisco Chronicle*

"One of science fiction's masters."

—*Starlog*

"Anderson has produced more milestones in contemporary science fiction and fantasy than any one man is entitled to; but he writes with such integrity and imagination that it's impossible to begrudge him either the esteem of his readers or the admiration of his peers."

—Stephen R. Donaldson

"One of hard science fiction's most consistently impressive writers."

—*Omni*

"Poul puts us into a whole new world."

—Larry Niven

"The great canvas of interstellar space comes alive under his hand as it does under no other."

—Gordon R. Dickson

"He has proven himself to be the master of the science fiction novel. . . . Anderson has clearly moved himself to the front and center of the science fiction corps."

—Jerry Pournelle

## BY POUL ANDERSON
## FROM TOM DOHERTY ASSOCIATES

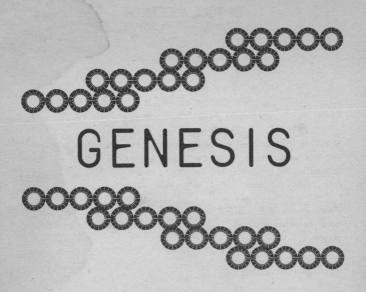

# GENESIS

## Poul Anderson

A TOM DOHERTY ASSOCIATES BOOK
NEW YORK

This is a work of fiction. All the characters and events portrayed in this book are either products of the author's imagination or are used fictitiously.

GENESIS

A Tor Book
Published by Tom Doherty Associates, LLC
175 Fifth Avenue
New York, NY 10010

www.tor.com

Tor® is a registered trademark of Tom Doherty Associates, LLC.

ISBN: 0-812-58028-1

First edition: February 2000
First mass market edition: February 2001

Printed in the United States of America

0 9 8 7 6 5 4 3 2 1

To Greg Bear, Gregory Benford, and David Brin,

Killer Bees and cosmic craftsmen

# PART ONE

To follow knowledge like a sinking star,

Beyond the utmost bound of human thought.

-ALFRED, LORD TENNYSON

The story is of a man, a woman, and a world. But ghosts pass through it, and gods. Time does, which is more mysterious than any of these.

A boy stood on a hilltop and looked skyward. The breeze around him was a little cold, as if it whispered of the spaces yonder. He kept his parka hood up. Gloves didn't make his fingers too clumsy for the telescope he had carried here. Already now, before the autumnal equinox, summer was dying out of the Tanana valley and the nights lengthening fast. Some warmth did linger in the forest that enclosed this bare height: he caught a last faint fragrance of spruce.

The dark reached brilliant above him, the Milky Way cleaving it with frost, the Great Bear canted and Capella outshining Polaris in the north, ruddy Arcturus and Altair flanking steely Vega in the west, a bewilderment of stars. Though the moon was down, treetops lifted gray beneath their light.

A spark rose among them, a satellite in a high-inclination orbit. The boy's gaze followed it till it vanished. Longing shook him. To be out there!

He would. Someday he would.

Meanwhile he had this much heaven. Best get started. He must flit back home at a reasonable hour. Tomorrow his school gyroball team was having practice, he wanted to work out a few more Fourier series—if you just told the computer to do it, you'd never learn what went on—and in the evening he'd take a certain girl to a dance. Maybe afterward he'd have nerve enough to recite her a poem he'd written about her. He hastily postponed that thought.

His astronomical pursuits had gone well past the usual sights. This time he savored their glories only briefly, for he was after a couple of Messier objects. There was no need to spoil the adaptation of his eyes. He spoke a catalogue number to the telescope mount. It found the RA and dec, pointed the instrument, and commenced tracking. He bent over the eyepiece and touched the knobs. Somehow it always felt better to focus for himself.

The thing swam into view, dim and misty. He hadn't the power to resolve more than a hint of structure. But it wasn't a nebula, it was a galaxy, the most remote he had yet tried for, suns in their tens of billions, their births and deaths, whirling neutron globes, unfathomable black holes, clouds of star-stuff, surely planets and moons and comets, surely—oh, please—living creatures, maybe—who could say?—some that were gazing his way and wondering.

*No. Stupid,* the boy chided himself. *It's too far. How many light-years? I can't quite remember.*

He didn't immediately ask for the figure. Down south he had seen the Andromeda glimmer awesome through six lunar diameters of arc, and it was a couple of million off. Here he spied on another geological era.

No, not even that. Lately he had added geology to his interests, and one day realized that magnolias were blooming on Earth when the Pleiades kindled. It strengthened his sense of the cosmos as a unity, where he too belonged. Well, that star cluster was only about a hundred parsecs away. (Only!) It was not altogether ridiculous to imagine what might be going on there as you watched, three and a quarter centuries after the light now in your eyes had departed it. But across gulfs far less deep than this that confronted him, simultaneity had no meaning whatsoever. His wistfulness to know if any spirit so distant shared his lifetime would never be quenched. It *could* not be.

The night chill seemed to flow through aperture and lens into him. He shivered, straightened, glanced around in a sudden, irrational search for reassurance.

Air tingled through his nostrils. Blood pulsed. The forest stood tall from horizon to horizon. Another satellite skittered low above it. An owl hooted.

The ground stayed firm beneath his feet. A nearby boulder, weathered, probably glacier-scarred, bore the same witness to abidingness. If human science asked its age, the answer would be as real as the stone.

*We're not little bits of nothing,* the boy thought half defiantly. *We count too. Our sun is a third as old as the universe. Earth isn't much younger. Life on Earth isn't much younger than that. And we have learned this all by ourselves.*

The silence of the stars replied: You have measured it. Do you understand it? Can you?

*We can think it,* he declared. *We can speak it, Can you?*

Why did the night seem to wait?

*Oh, yes,* he thought, *we don't see or feel it the way we do what's right around us. If I try to picture bricks or something side by side, my limit is about half a dozen. If I'd been counting since I was born and kept on till I died, I wouldn't get as high as twenty billion. But I reason. I imagine. That's enough.*

He had always had a good head for figures. He could scale them down till they lay in his mind like pebbles in his hand. Even those astrophysical ages—No, maybe it didn't make sense either, harking clear back to the quantum creation. Too much that was too strange had happened too fast. But afterward time must have run for the first of the stars as it did for him. The chronology of life was perfectly straightforward.

Not that it had an exact zero point. The traces were too faint. Besides, most likely there wasn't any such moment. Chemistry evolved, with no stage at which you could say *this* had come alive. Still, animate matter certainly existed sometime between three and a half and four billion years ago.

The boy's mind jumped, as if a meteor had startled him. *Let's split the difference and call the date three-point-six-five billion B.C.E.*, he thought. *Then one day stands for ten million years. Life began when January the first did, and this is midnight December the thirty-first, the stroke of the next new year.*

So . . . along about April, single cells developed, nuclei, ribosomes, and the rest. The cells got together, algae broke oxygen free into the atmosphere, and by November the first trilobites were crawling over the sea floor. Life invaded the land around Thanksgiving. The dinosaurs appeared early in December. They perished on Christmas Day. The hominids parted company with the apes at noon today. Primitive Homo sapiens showed up maybe fifteen minutes ago. Recorded history had lasted less than one minute. And here they were, measuring the universe, ranging the Solar System, planning missions to the stars.

*Where will we be by sunrise?* he wondered for a dizzying moment.

It passed. The upward steepness was an illusion, he knew. To go from worm to fish took immensely longer than to go from fish to mammal because the changes were immensely greater. By comparison, an ancient insectivore was very like an ape, and an ape nearly identical with a human.

*Just the same,* the boy thought, *we've become a force of nature, and not only on this world. It's never seen anything like us before. Our little piece of extra brain tissue has got to have taken us across a threshold.*

*But what threshold, and what's beyond it?*

He shivered again, pushed the question away from him, and turned back to his stargazing.

Strictly speaking, he was mistaken. In no particular was humankind unique. Nearly all animals had language, in the sense of communication between each other; among some, parts of it were learned, not innate, and actual dialects could develop. Many were technologists, in the sense of constructing things. A few used tools, in the sense of employing foreign objects for special tasks. A very few made tools, in the sense of slightly reshaping the objects; three or four species did this with the help of something besides their own mouths or digits.

Yet none came near to humans in any of these ways. In no other lineage did language grow so rich and powerful, for in them it sprang from an unprecedented capability of abstraction and reason. They had been toolmasters *par excellence* since before they were fully human; fire, chipped stone, and cut wood became conditions of their further evolution. At last the scope of their technology was such that natural selection no longer had significant effect on them. Like social insects and various sea dwellers, they were so well fitted to their surroundings that they bade fair to continue unaltered for millions of years. In their case, however, they themselves created—or were—their own environment. We can, if we like, say they had crossed a threshold.

Then we must say that another, more fateful one lay ahead.

For technology was never static. It continued to develop, at an ever more furious pace. Technological evolution was radically different from biological. It was not Darwinian, driven by contingency, competition, and a blind urge to reproduce. It was Lamarckian, driven by purpose. Its units of inheritance were not genes but memes—ideas, concepts, deliberately mutated or kept intact according to foreseen needs.

Knowledge also grew, in a fashion more nearly organic and haphazard until technology made science, the systematic search for verifiable information, possible. Thereafter the two nourished one another and the pace accelerated further.

More and more it was as though technology took on a life of its own, acting independently and ruthlessly. Gunpowder brought whole societies down. The steam engine forced basic change upon whole civilizations. Its internal-combustion successor turned the planet into a single quarrelsome neighborhood, while powering an agriculture that fed billions but starved what was left of the natural world. Computers remade industry, economics, and the everyday well-nigh beyond recognition, undermined liberty, and opened a road to space. The Internet, founded as a link between military centers, spread across the globe in a matter of years, revolutionized communication and access to knowledge like nothing since movable type, curbed tyrannies, and vexed governments everywhere. Automation made traditional skills useless, raising resentment and despair side by side with new wealth and new hopes.

"Artificial intelligence" was the name given the qualities of the most advanced systems. Certain of these went into the business of enhancing artificial intelligence. Soon the business was entirely theirs.

The boy became a man. For a while he adventured on Earth, then he went into space as he had dreamed.

The machines evolved onward.

Long afterward—almost unimaginably long afterward—Christian Brannock recalled that day. For it had been somehow both an ending and a beginning.

He did not see this until he looked back on his life and his afterlife in fullness. At the time, he was wholly caught up in the there and then. It was not even day, except by a clock set to North American hours; and at the moment Earth was some hundred million kilometers to starward, while night still lay over Clement Base.

Morning approached, but slowly. Between sunrise and sunrise, 176 terrestrial rotations passed. Not that the men here had ever gazed directly at a sunlit landscape on Mercury. Though a darkened pane might bring the brightness down to something endurable, other radiation would strike through. Their machines above ground ranged for them. Most of these were robots, with different degrees of autonomy. One was more.

Gimmick never knew darkness. Across five hundred kilometers, Christian saw by laserlight, radarlight, amplified starlight. He felt with fingers and tendrils of metal, with sensors in the treads as the body rolled across the regolith, with subtle seismics. He tasted and smelled with flickery beams of electrons and nuclear particles. He listened electronically to whispers of radioactivity from the rock around and to the hiss and

spatter of cosmic rain. Interior sensors kept him sublim-
inally aware of balances, flows, needs, as nerves and
glands did in his own body. Together, he and Gimmick
made observations and decisions, like his brain alone in
its skull; they moved the machine as his muscles moved
himself.

Rapport was not total. It could only be so in line-of-
sight. Relay, whether by satellite or by spires planted
along the way, inevitably reduced the bandwidth and
degraded the signal. Christian remained dimly conscious of his surroundings, the recliner in which he lay
connected, meters and instruments, air odorless and a
little chilly, tensions and easings—instinctive responses,
which sometimes made him strain against his bonds.
From the corner of an eye he glimpsed Willem Schuyten
seated at a control console, monitoring what went on.
That had seldom been necessary elsewhere, Christian
thought vaguely. Or, at least, he'd avoided it. But this
was a team effort, and on Mercury the unknowns were
many and the stakes high.

It was just half a minute's distraction, while Gimmick
did some data analysis that he couldn't follow. A certain
direction of search seemed promising, and the explorer
set off again. Christian's whole attention returned to
the scene.

Heaven glimmered and shimmered, its manifold bril-
liances arcing down to a horizon that on the left was
near and sharp. Craters pocked the murky terrain, boul-
ders lay strewn. When he glanced at any, he could tell
its age within a few million years, as he could tell the
age of a person or a tree on Earth; the clues were countless, the deductions subconscious. Close on the right a
scarp four kilometers high, hundreds of kilometers long,
loomed like a wall across the world. The enhancement
that was Christian-Gimmick perceived it as more than

rock. He noted traces as he went along; brain and computer joined to read the history, the tale of a gigantic upthrust along a fault line long ago when the planet was still cooling and shrinking after its birth.

He spied possibilities in something ahead.

Gimmick was following the cliff southwesterly, back toward the polar region where Clement waited. Rubble scrunched beneath the treads, soundlessly to human ears; dust smoked up and fell quickly down, under low gravity but unhindered by air. It did not cling to the robot, whose material repelled it.

*There,* Christian thought, *that crag yonder. Maybe a good anchor point. We'll have a look.* The partnership veered slightly and trundled nearer the heights. Debris lay deep here. Shards slipped aside. Motors labored. He considered deploying the six legs but decided that wasn't needful.

The peak sheered out of a lower slope above the rubble, a rough-edged hundred-meter obelisk. He had seen others as he traveled, though none so large. Probably shock-wave resonances in the age of uplift had split them from the massif.

He visualized this one as an almost ready-made core for a transmission tower, part of the global network that was to collect the solar energy cataracting down onto Mercury's dayside and hurl it out to orbiting antimatter factories—ultimately, to the laser beams that would send the first starships on their way! Passion thrummed in him.

*A quick structural exam. The self-robots can map the details later.* A disc at the end of an arm snugged tightly. Vibrations through stone returned their echoes, bearing tales.

The stone gave way. Thunder and blindness crashed down.

## 2

*"Wat drommel?"* Willem Schuyten cried. He went back to the expedition's English. "What the hell?" After a glance at the other man's face: "Hell indeed."

"N-no." Secured in the system, Christian Brannock could neither lift a braceleted arm nor shake his helmeted head. His voice shuddered. "Hold on. Keep going. Let me try to find out—what's happened—"

Willem nodded and concentrated on his instruments. Grown gray in the artificial intelligence field, he could make inferences from these readings and computations that might well escape an on-site observer.

Shards and tatters of input went through Christian like a nightmare, blackness, deafness, crushing heaviness, powers lost, strength in ebb. Instinct panicked; his flesh struggled against the restraints. But somehow his mind clung to the steadiness that was Gimmick's. Together they tried to interpret what little the sensors gave them.

Those fitful moments of reality turned more and more chaotic. They weakened, too, until he could not make out whatever form they still had.

*The linkage is failing fast. Better break it altogether and start work.* Christian never knew whether the decision was his alone or rooted also in his partner's calm logic. Nor did he know or care why it ended with: *So long. Good luck.*

"Terminate," he rasped aloud.

"Terminate," Willem repeated. He swept a glance and a judgment across the gauges, deemed that an immediate breakoff was neurologically safe, and pressed the command button. Voice-activated, the communication center could have done everything by itself, but a human in the loop was an added precaution. He could better tell what another human required.

All channels shut down. The neuroconnectors released Christian. He lay for a minute breathing hard, then sat up. Willem stood above him with a tumbler of water. Christian drained it in two gulps. "Thanks," he mumbled. "Dry as yon landscape, my mouth was."

"Terror will do that," his companion replied. "I saw your involuntary reactions. Want a levozine?"

Christian half grinned, without merriment. "What I really want is a stiff drink. But we're in a hurry. Yes, I'll take a pill."

Willem gave him one. Some were always on hand, in case a mission got unexpectedly long or difficult and the operator could not stop to rest. "In a hurry, you said? Do you mean there is something we can do at once?"

Christian nodded. "We'd bloody well better." He climbed to his feet. The medication began to tranquilize and stimulate. His trembling died away, his voice gained force. "Whew! Hope I can snatch a shower during preparations. I smell six weeks dead, don't I?" Sweat sheened on his skin and darkened his shirt.

Willem regarded him narrowly. "My monitors say the machine is a ruin. The transceiver's badly damaged. It can carry some information, erratically, but the power unit's out of commission. Anything that could perhaps function, like an arm, can't anymore. And the energy reserve is dwindling fast."

"Gimmick's intact."

Willem sighed. "Yes, evidently. That hurts, doesn't it?" He had often heard such highly developed computers and neural nets, with their programs and databases, called "brains." People who worked with one, like Christian—although seldom as intimately as he did—were apt to give it a name and speak of its personal quirks, as other people might speak of a ship or a tool that had served them a long time. "I imagine you'd prefer the wreck to have been quick and total. Merciful, so to speak. That would have been a shock to you, however, worse than you got."

"I know. Like suddenly dying myself. I'd have recovered. But this way—My God, man, Gimmick's out there, not a heap of smashed parts but Gimmick! And sunrise is coming."

Willem sighed. "Exactly. Have you any idea what happened?"

The question, its style carefully parched, demanded an answer in kind. Christian's fists unclenched. "We were examining an unusual sort of crag. All at once it broke into huge chunks. It buried Gimmick." His tone sharpened. "The body Gimmick was using." Again impersonal: "The top of the transceiver mast, with the dish, is sticking out, and what came to me shows that the interior armor protected the brain."

"Are you sure? It could be in poor shape too."

Christian shook his head. "No. Do you believe I wouldn't know that, feel it, same as I would if my own brain took a concussion?"

"All right. But the accident—how could a collapse happen? An earthquake?"

"No." Christian spoke with certainty. He had, in a way, been there. "Nor a meteorite strike. Somehow our seismic probe must have touched things off. I don't see how. You know it didn't have any great force. And Mercury's geologically used up. That jut of rock stood unchanged for—what?—three billion years?"

"A freak occurrence, then."

"Maybe. Or maybe such formations and weaknesses are common. How much do we know? Why the devil are we on Mercury, except to get the lay of the land? Before something like this happens elsewhere—"

Christian drew breath and forced coolness upon himself. "I was only in linkage with Gimmick. The full information isn't in me, it's in his database. If we don't retrieve him before sunrise, everything will be baked and blasted to nothing."

"I suppose so. Thermostatic system destroyed and the rocks probably not a good replacement for smashed radiation shielding." Willem laid a hand on his friend's shoulder. "I'm sorry. Dreadful luck. Worse for you than the expedition, perhaps. This association you've grown used to, this particular rapport you've developed, gone. You'll have to start all over, won't you?" He regarded the creases in the face, the fallowness in the blond hair. "Unless you choose to make a career change, or just retire. I'm sorry, Christian."

The response lashed at him: "No! There's time to go dig, detach Gimmick from the wreckage, get back here. But we've got to move, I tell you!"

"I . . . am afraid not. Let me check and make sure." Willem turned to his keyboards and readouts. Christian stood where he was. His fists doubled again.

After a while the cyberneticist looked at him and said slowly: "No. I've gathered the present whereabouts of everything we have with proper capability," self-programming robots surveying and studying the planet in advance of the grand enterprise. Christian's had been the only direct human-machine alliance, expensive in terms of life support and equipment, rewarding in terms of special situations calling for an organic mind on the scene. "They're scattered across the globe, remember. Even the nearest has rough terrain to cross. None can get there soon enough."

Christian had become quite composed. "I guessed so. Well, it isn't too far from here. I'll go myself."

# 3

Everyone else at Clement called the idea insane. The central artificial intelligence made a lightning-quick calculation and agreed. No possible gain was worth the risk of losing the outfit necessary, let alone a human life. Commander Gupta forbade it.

Christian Brannock stood his ground. He and Gimmick had been doing work impossible for any single man or machine. The delay while a replacement was found and brought to the planet, then the time spent regaining the lost information, could possibly cripple the whole undertaking, if only by the added cost. More to the point, as an independent contractor he had broad discretion. Within limits that he insisted he was not exceeding, he could commandeer whatever he needed to cope with an emergency.

His haste and resolution overbore them. Two hours later he was on his way.

After that, he waited. The rover that carried him operated itself. Its program included a topographic map, and survey satellites provided exact detail. Following its progress through communication relays, from time to time the intelligence at base ordered a change of course that would make for better speed. None of this impinged directly on Christian. Nor could he talk with the robot that accompanied him. It was built for power and dexterity, not thought. When they reached the site, the intelligence would direct its operations. Meanwhile its bulk crowded a cabin intended for, at most, three men.

Otherwise he was fairly comfortable. Air blew recycled, always pure. (He remembered odors of blossoms, pines, a woman's sunlit hair.) Temperature varied subtly because that was best for health and alertness, without regard to the hundred-kelvin cold of midnight or the searing three hundred Celsius degrees of noonday. (He remembered a beach where surf burst and roared, a wind chill in his face and salt on his lips but warmth radiant from a leeward bluff.) The metal around him hummed and quivered, the deck underfoot pitched and swayed, as the vehicle drove full tilt across a rugged land. However, the seat in which he sat harnessed compensated for most, and what it could not entirely counteract didn't amount to much in Mercurian gravity. If anything, the motion soothed, almost cradlelike. (He remembered a boat heeled over, climbing the crests of waves and diving into their troughs, the tiller athrum beneath his hand, the mainsail a snowpeak against heaven.)

Exhaustion claimed him. He ate and drank something, reclined the seat, and slept. His dreams were uneasy. Once during them he asked Gimmick, "Do you ever dream? When we're not linked, I mean," and the robot replied, "You taught me how." Or was that a confused memory? They'd been together quite a few years, in quite a few strange places.

He woke refreshed, though, unharnessed, balanced himself against the lurching while he stretched his muscles and used the sanitor, ate more of the cold rations, and settled back down. When he called for a revised estimate of arrival time, the vehicle said "About another three hours" in its flat voice.

He frowned. That wouldn't be long before sunrise. Well, he'd known when he started that this was the best he could hope for. And . . . the swollen solar disc would take fifteen hours to clear the horizon.

He looked outward. Direct vision was impossible when he sat in the middle of thick armor, but the electronics that he activated gave him a simulacrum as good. Suddenly it was as if everything above the deck were gone and he directly beneath the sky, naked, alone, invulnerable. So might an angel have seen.

No, only a man. He did not now share the more than human senses of his partner. But for a while he lost himself in unaided vision.

A kind of dawn was breaking in the northeast, zodiacal light strengthened by the nearness of the sun. It lifted above rocks and craters like a huge wing, softly pearl-hued, a quarter of the way to the zenith before it faded among stars. The galactic belt outshone it, an ice-bright river from worldedge to worldedge. Everywhere else the stars themselves gleamed and glittered, their thousands overwhelming the crystalline blackness behind. Though Christian had beheld them oftener than he could recall, for a moment he felt his spirit fall free, upward and upward forever into the majesty of their silence.

A glimpse drew him back. Low over a northwesterly ridge stood a blue diamond. He could just espy a mote beside it, ashen-gold. Earth, he knew, and Earth's moon. Home.

Did that moon tonight throw a glint off a bit of Ellen's windborne dust?

Sometimes, without warning, the memory of her overtook him. He had long since healed himself of grief. There had been women before her, there had been women afterward. But she was the one for whom he left space and settled down to groundside engineering, because nothing was worth leaving her for months or years on end. When she died—robotic controls could not yet prevent every senseless accident—and he had scattered the contents of the urn across the countryside she loved, he returned to space. Their son was grown and didn't need him any longer. He took up the new technology of human-machine linkage, and seldom came back for a visit. But from time to time he remembered, and it hurt.

Maybe, selfishly speaking, he was otherwise better off. Of course, he'd been happy to pay the price. Nevertheless, on Earth he had always felt trapped. The stars—

Again he looked aloft. A deeper longing shook him. He had fared and wrought across the Solar System. Beyond waited a universe.

Half angrily, he dismissed the emotion. Self-pity. They were going to the stars, yes, but it wouldn't happen in his lifetime, and they wouldn't be flesh and blood, they would be machines. Oh, sentient, sensitive, bearing with them all the heritages of history, but not really human.

Her ghost lingered. It made the cabin too quiet.

He was not mawkish. In his job, he couldn't be and survive. Yet you couldn't survive either if you were a dullard. That meant you found ways to occupy long, empty stretches of time—not merely games and recorded shows, but anything from acquiring a language or mastering calligraphy to creating an artwork or maturing a philosophy. Christian Brannock was, among other things, a ballad singer who had composed several of his own.

He had taken his guitar along. The optics of total outervision obscured his immediate surroundings, but he knew where it was racked. He reached and pulled it free. Sound-board and strings glimmered into sight as he laid it over his lap. He struck a chord and began to sing.

*"Once upon a hearth*
*We lit a little fire*
*To warm our winter hands*

*And kindle our desire,*
*Which never needed this;*
*But still, we found it good*
*To see the flames seduce*
*The dry and virgin wood.—"*

No. The music clanged to a halt. He had made the song in his Earthside youth, later Ellen enjoyed it, a while ago he revived it on Mars, where no true flame had ever danced. Doing it here felt somehow wrong.

Why was he so churned up inside? Because he was in danger of losing Gimmick? But Gimmick was only a machine, wasn't he—wasn't it? Well, maybe not "only." . . .

Christian had work to make ready for. Defiantly, he launched into something older and bawdier.

*"Oh, a tinker came a-strolling,*
*A-strolling down the Strand—"*

## 4

Already the solar corona was well over a ridge in the northeast. Its opalescent glory drowned the zodiacal light and cast a wan, shadowful glow across pocks and scars beneath. A crimson tongue of prominence heralded the oncoming disc. Elsewhere the stars still ruled. Earth no longer beckoned. The scarp blocked sight of it.

That cliff sheered from horizon to horizon, filling nearly half the sky. Christian remembered ledges, pinnacles, steeps, mineral streaks, the mark of meteorite strikes through billions of years. But he had seen those together with Gimmick. To his unaided eyes the heights were one vast darkness.

He might have imagined they were a storm front—on its own timescale the cosmos is neither enduring nor peaceful, it is appallingly violent—except that the wreckage on the rubble slope at the foot gripped his attention. His partner lay below that heap of broken stone. The communication disc poked above. He couldn't make out exactly what damage it had suffered. Besides, lacking the necessary connectors, he was cut off from it. However, the intelligence back at Clement Base had no such limitations.

"Are you in touch?" he cried to it through the rover's radio. "What can you tell us?"

The voice that replied was baritone. It could be in any register, always as vibrant and expressive as any human's. "No more than formerly. The robot does not respond to calls. Evidently its own signals would be too feeble and distorted, and it doesn't waste energy trying. Internal power is barely sufficient to maintain computational functions."

*In other words, Gimmick remains conscious,* Christian said to himself. *No, I'm being anthropomorphic. Which isn't scientific, is it?* "Does he know we're here?"

"Possibly, through seismic or electronic traces." The intelligence put a note of urgency into its calm. "Don't delay if you want to save anything that matters."

Christian thought of Gimmick lying prisoned, waiting either for rescue or death. Sensing? Hoping? So had many humans done, when an earthquake buried them alive or a disabled spacecraft went helpless off on trajectory. Was it altogether fantastic to suppose that Gimmick wanted to live?

"Right," he said. "Take over the robot." He hesitated. "Please."

The big, half manlike thing stirred. It turned about and rumbled from the cabin. Christian heard its mass reach the crew-access airlock, then after a minute the hiss of pumps evacuating the chamber. He saw it go forth onto the surface, into the coronal luminance, stand for another minute while the intelligence at Clement studied the scene through its sensors, and start climbing the talus. Shards slipped from beneath its feet and slid downward. On Earth they would have rattled.

He couldn't endure to sit and watch. His assigned part came toward the end, when he applied tools for which the robot was not designed. But the corona was creeping higher, the flame-tongue standing taller. Maybe his slight strength would make the slight difference that counted.

The intelligence perceived. "Don't," it warned. "You will hazard yourself more than enough according to plan."

"I'm the captain here," Christian flung back.

On the way out he stopped by a locker. From the geological gear stored there he took a pick and spade. At the lock he donned his spacesuit and went through his checklist with the almost mindless ease of long practice. *Almost* mindless; one tiny malfunction or mistake could kill you. Machines were hardier. No wonder that it would be they who went to the stars. By now there weren't too many uses for humans even on the planets.

Gear and all, he weighed less than he did unclad on Earth. Inertia was the same, of course, a combination that could get tricky. He bounded across the ground to the detritus slope, but therefore picked his way with care. From the top he caught a chiaroscuro view of the rover, its metal partly shadowed, partly agleam under the waxing radiance. If you ignored details, it looked rather like a giant version of Gimmick's body, minus the specialized limbs, detectors, and collection bins—an ovoid with a turret, legs currently folded while it rested on caterpillar treads, radiator fins deployed against the sun's assault.

To hell with bodies. Gimmick had worn a lot of different bodies. What needed saving was the unitized hardware, software, and database. The brain. The mind? The soul? Anyway, Gimmick himself.

The robot toiled stolidly. Attachments on its four arms loosened rocks and flung them off, to bounce across the lower terrain. Often it paused while the intelligence considered, then moved to another spot. Christian knew this was to excavate efficiently and avoid causing a slide. His judgment was poor by comparison, his muscles weak. Nevertheless, if he was cautious he could help rather than hinder—help just a bit.

The body began to appear, cruelly battered and rent. The corona climbed.

Christian dug. After a while he gasped. The spacesuit's equilibrators couldn't quite keep up; his faceplate fogged, his air thickened and stank. Hands trembled on handles. "Conserve yourself," advised the serene voice. "You'll be wanted for a precision task."

He yielded. To stop his labor was about as hard a thing as he could recall ever doing.

A sliver of sun blazed over the ridge. Suddenly shadows were long and sharp. Small craters stood out of them like atolls. Stars fled from eyesight.

Fifteen hours . . . But well before then, the solar wind would sweep across the land, bearing its radiation rain. Furnace heat would follow. Only in the rover was there refuge.

"If you are prudent, you will retreat," said the voice.

"I know," Christian answered. "I ain't."

The robot worked on.

The midsection emerged. If Christian's faceplate had not been self-darkening, the light off it would have blinded him. But he could at last get to his real job.

Nearly level, the sunbeams were little diffused. Night still hung around whatever they did not strike directly. The tool kit secured to his suit included provisions such as flashbeams and miniradars, but often he had to go by touch, through sensory-amplifying power gloves. The objective was to open several layered shells and detach the independent unit, as delicately as a brain surgeon.

"The background count is rising fast," said the intelligence.

"Shut up," said Christian. "I'm busy."

And somehow he freed Gimmick before either of them took too large a dose. He cradled the spheroid and its trailing cables in his arms, he crept down the rubble slope and leaped across the regolith. Dust puffed from his boots. The airlock opened for him. He stumbled through and up to the cabin, where he collapsed into a seat. His heart thuttered. As yet, the turmoil in him drowned any feeling of triumph. Mostly he lusted for a cold beer. Or two or three or four.

The robot spent a while examining the discarded machine and selecting rock specimens before it joined him. It had no reason to hurry.


5


Like Christian, Gimmick need not be in rapport in order to process data and execute a program—to remember, think, be aware. Unlike him, it did not need a body for this. A power supply and a few input-output connections sufficed. Upon returning, it had been linked to the central intelligence for purposes of downloading and analyzing the knowledge it brought. Those circuits were now inoperative.

The voice from the intercom should therefore have been flat, the words an unemotional report. To mimic humanness as well as the central intelligence did required capabilities beyond any called for in an explorer—especially an explorer that would often be under the guidance of a human mind. Yet tone and language this day carried more than bare information. Something else, a hint as of life, flowed along.

"You've found the cause of the collapse?" Christian asked eagerly.

"Uh-huh," replied Gimmick. "The nanotech studied crystal structures atom by atom, and then the big brain set up a model and ran it. It turns out this particular mineral combination is unusually vulnerable to thermal stress. Oh, not much, or the crag wouldn't have stood so long. But gigayears of heat and cold, heat and cold chewed on it. Solar wind and cosmic rays didn't help. Flaws developed and grew till any substantial shock would bring everything tumbling down. Sooner or later, a good-sized meteorite would have hit nearby."

Christian frowned. "We gave it no such push."

"Sure, our seismic probe was gentle. But the resonant frequencies were enough. Construction or a spacecraft landing in the neighborhood would have done the same."

"How great a problem will this be?"

"We'll have to find out. Probably not very. The rock doesn't appear to be a common sort. In any case, the planners will be forewarned."

"I daresay the business was worth what it cost, then. But we're earning our pay!"

Did the voice quiver, ever so faintly? "When can we start surveying again?"

"Don't know. I've looked into the matter, and it isn't practical to modify any robot on the planet for you. If making a new body and shipping it from Earth will take too long, I'll negotiate early termination of our contract and let another team succeed us. I don't want to sit idled for months, above all on Mercury." Christian glanced at Willem Schuyten. "Sorry," he murmured. "Nothing wrong with the company here."

The older man smiled wryly. "Aside from a lack of live women. I don't especially care for virtuals."

"And the rest of the universe waiting," Christian said, more softly still.

The cyberneticist gave him a look that went deep. For a moment the room lay silent. It was Christian's quarters. At present, one wall screen held a view of Saturn in space, jewel-exquisite. In another, dry snow drifted across a flank of Everest, white beneath lordly blue. A third, smaller, displayed a portrait of his Ellen, which he seldom animated anymore, and a fourth had the likeness of their son, which he often did. His guitar leaned against a desk cluttered with figurines and the equipment for creating them. A bottle and two tumblers stood companionably on the table between the men.

Christian stirred. "Well," he said toward the intercom, "I'll let you know as soon as I do myself. Meanwhile, if you've nothing to keep you amused, I expect you'll turn yourself off. Adios."

"Until then," responded the voice, and ceased.

"Escape from boredom," Christian muttered. "I envy you that."

"Do you really?" asked Willem almost as low.

Christian paused before he replied. "I suppose not. Envy wouldn't make sense, would it?"

"Not envy of a machine. But you spoke with Gimmick the way one speaks with a friend."

Christian shrugged. "Habit. Haven't you ever talked or sworn at a machine?"

"I said 'spoke with,' not 'spoke at.' It never struck me before—I never was exposed to it so directly—how you two *converse*. How eerily lifelike Gimmick sounded. How much like you."

"I shouldn't think you'd be surprised. You're the expert on AI."

"It's an enormous field, and enlarging exponentially. I had no experience with your sort of team until I came to Mercury. And of course my work here has been with the main system," helping it direct the manifold activities on a world full of unknowns.

"But I mean, it's so obvious. Gimmick's not a thing I steer like a boat or put on and take off like a glove. He can operate by himself. He makes judgments and acts on them. He learns. Naturally he'd learn—pick up traits—from me."

"And you from him," Willem said slowly.

Christian's hand, reaching for his drink, dropped to the table and doubled into a fist. "I never thought I'd hear that out of *your* mouth," he snapped. " 'Dehumanization,' 'emotional deprivation,' all the Organicist quack-quackery infesting Earth."

Willem raised his own palm. "Peace, I pray. I certainly do know better. No offense intended. My apologies."

Christian relaxed somewhat. "I'm sorry. Overreaction, stupid of me." He gave the other a rueful smile. "After that go-around at the scarp, I guess my nerves haven't yet stopped jangling."

"Very understandable. But I do want to make a point, and then . . . lead up to something that's been more and more on my mind."

Christian lifted the tumbler, sipped, and leaned back in his chair. "Go ahead, do."

"You've given Gimmick a name, jocular, but doesn't that in itself show a feeling? And you persistently refer to Gimmick not as 'it' but 'he.'"

"Sure. Why not? I've owned a couple of boats on Earth, named them, and called them 'she.'"

"But you said it yourself, Gimmick is not a passive piece of machinery. Within . . . his . . . limits, to all intents and purposes, he thinks. In linkage with you, he becomes . . . an aspect, a facet of a human being."

"No," Christian said quietly. "In linkage, together, we're more than human."

"In sensory range, in capabilities, yes. Which is bound to affect you. But you are the man. Yours are the instincts, drives, fears and hopes, joys and sorrows, everything that four billion years of evolution on Earth has made. Do you imagine contact with that would not affect him?"

Again Christian gathered his thoughts before he answered. "Of course it has. During the time we've worked as a team, and that's been a spell now, I've noticed. And not been surprised." He tossed off a dram. "That's part of why I get so angry at those snotheads. Robotization of humans? How about humanization of robots?"

"Within their limits, as you put it," Willem said carefully.

Christian nodded. "Agreed. I don't pretend Gimmick is the equal of—of you. How can we compare . . . apples and bluebirds?"

"When you insisted on going out and risking your life, you claimed it was to save the data. They did prove to be important. However, what you really intended was to rescue your friend. Was it not?"

Christian sat silent.

Willem sighed. "Still, compared to the central intelligence here on Mercury, not to speak of the greater systems on Earth, Gimmick is very limited. And as I said, things are changing exponentially. Now I will soon be obsolete and retire to rusticate. Everybody like me will.

"Where will it end? Where does computational power leave off and actual consciousness begin? I don't know, and this field has been my lifelong specialty. Nobody knows, and they've been wondering about it for two or three centuries."

He leaned forward. His eyes sought Christian's and held fast. "But I do know a few things that are not yet public. You have heard of uploading entire personalities into a computer?"

"Who hasn't?" Christian retorted. "Isn't that another notion they've kicked around ever since when? Last analysis I saw, the idea was unworkable. Entropy . . ." Confronting the sudden intensity across the table, he let his words trail off.

"That was then," Willem said. "We've reached the truly steep part of the progress curve. Uploading should be possible within another ten or fifteen years. Scan the entire organism, transfer the informational matrix to a database in an advanced neural network, add sensors and effectors. Yes, a machine existence. But not like any ordinary or even extraordinary robot's. And maybe later—Who knows what will become possible later?

"If, by then, you want it."

Christian shivered. "Yes." Willem nodded. "I have been watching you and your partner. You strike me as an excellent candidate for uploading.

"The first starships should be ready not long after the end of your mortal life expectancy. The expeditions will need an element of human judgment, human will and desire. Think about it. Barring mishaps such as you have lately courted, you have time to decide. How would you like a continuation of you to go to the stars?"

# ∞  IV  ∞

No living man or woman ever went. Flesh is too frail.

Consider. Light *in vacuo* moves at the ultimate velocity, some three hundred thousand kilometers per second. Nothing can outrace it. For matter, that would require more than infinite energy; for information it would imply systems able to reach backward through time and alter the past that brought them into being.

In the era when the pioneer voyagers left Sol, light took four and a third years to traverse the distance to the next nearest sun. The average separation of stars in their outlying part of the galaxy was about twice that.

If an interplanetary mission was urgent, a spacecraft sometimes boosted to as high as a hundred kilometers per second. Thus it got from Earth to Mars in a minimum of ten days, to far Pluto in a year and a half. Such haste was extravagant of power, seldom used, and only by flyers of small mass. Otherwise robots fared at their leisure.

Given a speed like this, one could make the least of interstellar crossings in thirteen thousand years.

The central intelligence on Earth, linked to its subordinates and to its equals elsewhere in the Solar System, designed vessels more capable. It was scarcely necessary to test them once they were built—or, we might better say, grown. So profound was the intelligence's understanding of natural law and physical reality, so potent its logic and mathematics. The Alpha Centauri expedition was only ten years under way. In due course it would be feasible to approach the speed of light.

Now, space is in fact not a vacuum. Hydrogen and helium gas pervade it, together with dust that here and there forms great clouds. Nowhere is this medium dense, except when a part falls in on itself and makes new stars. In Sol's region at that time it ran to approximately one atom per cubic centimeter. Yet anything moving at any substantial fraction of the ultimate velocity encounters many of them every second. Each collision releases energy. The hard radiation would kill an organic creature well-nigh instantly.

It was difficult enough to protect the electronics and photonics of the machines, or even their metal. Material shielding did not suffice. Besides producing secondary radiation, as bad as the primary or worse, it would soon be ablated away. Magnetohydrodynamic force fields were required, closely controlled, ever changeable according to need, as subtle as they were powerful. They too were incompatible with carbon-based life—which, in any case, demanded absurdly elaborate and massive apparatus for its maintenance.

Consciousness went to the stars: machine consciousness.

Watched from outside, that inaugural departure was a sight beautiful but hardly spectacular. An arrowlike shape, ashine in the light of the distant sun, glided from orbit and dwindled into heaven. Later an aureole surrounded it and trailed it, like an incandescent comet, though this was mainly at wavelengths beyond the visible. When it reached its goal it transmitted its discoveries and experiences back to the central intelligence and to any humans who cared.

Many did, often because the starfarer was not altogether alien. A robot aboard carried the spirit of Christian Brannock.

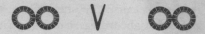

The countryside rolled in gentle hills, intensely green, starred with wildflowers. Trees stood alone or in small, widely strewn groves, oak, beech, elm. A breeze tossed light and shadow through their crowns. Looking out, Laurinda Ashcroft could almost feel warmth and wind, hear birdsong, breathe odors of growth.

But the view was electronic, for her house and its few neighbors lay underground. Nor was the nature above them ancient. A century ago this had been a plantation, broken here and there by the ruins of an ugly industrial town. Not until the useful genetically engineered monstrosities became obsolete was everything razed and a preserve created.

Yet above a ridge to the east rose a steeple, as it had for more than a thousand years.

*All this beauty can die again,* she thought, *crushed beneath ice, sickened and seared by radiation, or—who knows? Someday, somehow, by some or other cosmic chance, it must.* The knowledge saddened. *Unless, before then, Terra Central decides it's outlived its value.*

She recoiled from that idea, the sense of helplessness. *Never mind! Right now we only have to cope with the universe. Which means first coping with man.*

Will and strength rallied. She turned back to her visitor. He stood waiting for her to find words after his cautious greeting. The trace of a smile on his lips was like a flag of truce.

Not that Omar Hamid would recognize a symbol so archaic. Laurinda drew breath, formed a full smile herself, and bowed her head briefly over bridged fingers. He responded likewise. The modern gesture calmed her. The foreboding that his entry had roused died away as quickly as it had risen. It had been unreasonable. After all, he had called ahead, days in advance, and he was here simply to talk. She was surprised that meeting him could affect her so much.

"Yes, you're welcome, Omar," she said. "Always."

His shyness, if that was what it had been, hardened into a certain wariness. "In spite of my errand?" His Inglay was more accented than formerly. Perhaps he hadn't had many occasions to use it.

Laurinda shook her head. "In spite of its having been so long," she answered low.

"I'm sorry." It sounded genuine. "I thought you would rather not . . . see me again."

"True. For a while."

"And then?" The tone was half anxious.

"It stopped hurting. I remembered what was good. Otherwise—we made a mistake, you and I. An honest mistake, and we were very young."

The look he gave her was briefly, uncannily familiar. It was as if the wrinkles and the short white beard were a mask, gone transparent for a glimpse of the face she once knew.

"Sometimes I even wished you would call," she added.

"I hardly dared," he said.

"Me too. Although I think what we both feared most was pride, wounded youthful pride, each other's and our own."

"It would probably have been another mistake to try again."

"The same one, with the same result. Or still more bitter. But I did begin thinking, now and then, how nice it would be to hear from you."

"Likewise for me. Of course, I kept hearing *of* you, oftener and oftener. I hoped—I hope you've been happy."

"Why should I not have been?"

"Your life became so different."

Their gazes met and held steady, but somehow hers went through him, beyond this room and this moment. " 'A sea change,' " she murmured, " 'into something rich and strange.' "

*The living planet and the souls upon it. The knowledge, vision, wisdom, and presence of Terra Central. The minds at other stars, the stars themselves, the marvel and mystery that is the cosmos. And I amidst all these.*

Omar's question drew her back out of reverie. "What do you mean?"

"Oh, that," she said, carefully careless. "Only a quotation."

"Your style of talking has certainly changed. Scholarly, is that the word? I suppose working with Terra Central did it."

"Not really. I read a great deal." Laurinda formed a new smile. "Anachronistic habit, agreed."

But necessary, she had found—for her, at any rate, if not for everyone who served as an interface between human and machine. Those wonders were too great, those thoughts too high. She had been in danger of losing her own humanness to them. The works and songs of the past redeemed it. Sometimes that past, even its fictions—Hamlet, Anne Elliot, Wilkins Micawber, Vidal Benzaguen—felt closer to her than the world she lived in.

She broke off. "Enough," she said. "At least, enough about me. Do sit down, please. What refreshment can I offer? You used to like coffee, black, strong, and sweet."

"Thank you," Omar replied. "I still do." He paused. "Thank you for remembering."

Chairs shaped themselves to bodies with fluid, unnoticed sensuality. Laurinda gave the house an instruction. "Tell me about yourself," she urged her guest.

"You know." He spoke defensively.

"Just your recent activities. What did you do, how did you do, in the years between?"

He shrugged. "On the whole, contented. I pursued my interests—mainly sports, you know."

"I suppose you became a champion."

"Not quite, but I didn't do badly."

"I'm sorry. I should have followed the athletics news."

"No, no. I realize you've had too much other claim on your attention." Ruefulness: "Besides, that also is well behind me. Treatments, therapies, regenerations, the whole kit of somatics, can only hold off aging for so long." Again he regarded her, and she thought that what he saw pained him a little. He continued faster: "Games and contests haven't been everything. I've made a fair amount of yun both as a coach and as a personal counselor."

She raised her brows. "Yun?"

"Local slang. I've spent the past decade mainly on Taiwan. If you haven't happened to encounter the word, it means credit earned, over and above the basic issue. Do they still call it plusses in England?"

"Yes. I should have guessed. But I feel a bit overwhelmed today." Laurinda hesitated. "I don't want—to be impertinent—but—"

Omar chuckled, more nearly at ease than hitherto. "But you were never timid. Well, for the most part I've been happy. One orthomarriage lasted more than forty years. We were allowed two children. We chose girls." He must have seen her own quick pain; he must know she had never had any. Doubtless he assumed that was because, whatever her relationships with men, none had endured. Or did he go deeper and see that Terra Central had taken up too much of her time, of herself? He finished roughly: "And I've become active in public affairs."

She nodded. "Politics."

Scorn responded. "Not standing for election. What does any political office mean anymore? But advisory committees."

"That is today's main form of politics, isn't it? That, and working to create a general consensus on major issues."

"It's why I've come here."

"Certainly. Again, welcome, old friend."

The house recognized a psychological moment. A servitor glided in to set down the freshly synthesized coffee for him, tea for her, and small cakes. Incense wafted from a miniature brazier. As they partook they exchanged conventional remarks, empty of practical significance, full of emotional tones, two animals instinctively reassuring one another. This visit in person, from halfway around the globe, said more than any telepresence ever could.

When he ended the interlude, she sensed that he must force himself. "You know what I'll ask of you."

She looked away, off into one of the screens where the day outside shone. "Do you really believe I can grant it?"

"I can hope. It's not as if we were at a final decision

point. The debate may go on for years." His voice harshened. "Unless Terra Central strikes it down and orders an action."

Her head swung back towards him. She stiffened. "What makes you imagine that could happen?"

"I said it before. What force is left in the World Charter or the law of any state? We talk, we vote, we go solemnly through our traditional motions, but the decisions that matter come from the machine intelligences—at the summit, from Terra Central."

"Not decisions, not commands. Advice, which we do best to follow."

"You imply the world has become too complex, too precarious, for mere humans to understand and control."

"It always was, wasn't it?" she said quietly.

Taken aback, he sat mute for a while. Perhaps he reflected that her books must have given her more knowledge of the historical past, the terrible past, than most people had. At last he replied, "Well, facts, logic, models, calculations, yes, of course we need Terra Central, the whole cybernetic system. But what we want, what we feel, that counts for at least as much."

"She welcomes this input too."

He stared. "She . . . ?" he whispered.

"Just what do you wish of me?" Laurinda challenged.

"That you, today, speak for liberty. The last liberty we have. If those proposals go through, we'll lose it."

"I don't agree." Almost automatically, so often had she explained the viewpoint, she added, "True, if we take her counsel we'll have to accept certain changes. But largely it will be less a matter of anything compulsory than of giving up some things for the sake of the future. Some parklands must be converted, some volcanoes awakened, some installations built, a number of other programs carried out. To pay for this, a slight reduction in basic credit issue; there will be things we can't afford any longer, but, really, very minor. No worse. I honestly can't find sense in the claims your faction has been making."

"The changes won't be that minor. Nor the compulsions. Only think of the Siberian forest gone back to steppe, North Africa back to desert, lava burying the Gardens of Hawaii—all the loss of recreation, places to be alone in, to draw a free breath in. More than that, the condemning of property, the displacement of residents. When instead we can simply—"

She cut him off. "Please. We've both fallen into our set-piece speeches, haven't we? Let me just point out that there's nothing 'simply' about your scheme. It carries its own price. And the heaviest part of that price would fall on later generations who were never given a choice."

"Are you sure of that? They'll have had nine thousand years to make ready, in whatever way they themselves find best."

"No, I am not sure. *She* isn't. History is chaotic. Nobody and nothing can forecast what the situation, the possibilities and impossibilities, will be in another nine thousand years. We must secure these resources against that day, while we still definitely have them and have the means to use them."

Starkness yielded to sadness. "But why are we repeating these worn-out arguments, Omar? Did you actually believe you could convince me in two or three hours, or that I could then convince others?"

"It seemed worth trying," he admitted. "Your influence isn't negligible. Oh, obviously I can't change your basic opinion today, if ever. But I was hoping to persuade you to give ours honorable mention, to tell your audience they should listen to us and think seriously about what we have to say." His voice gathered passion. "Laurinda, I know you love all the life on Earth. But doesn't the freedom of that life—to cope for itself, to evolve—doesn't that matter too? Do you like the prospect of life turned into nothing but a, a pet, controlled down to the last cell by a machine?"

Stung, she snapped, "You know that's ridiculous."

The thought flitted through her, not for the first time: *Is it?* She struck back: "Carry it just a little further, and you may as well join the Stormseekers."

Memory rose against her will, of a rally in North America. She had seen a bit of it on the news and ordered a complete replay. The words rolled thunderous: "*—I say let the Ice come. It won't be the end of the world, it will be a strengthening and a liberation. Life was never more rich, more vigorous, than last time, in the Pleistocene, nor man more creative, more free. When Terra Central lies dead beneath the glacier, then from the cold tundras to the rainlands around the Equator, men will again make their own destinies.—*" The gathering cheered, applauded, waved banners aloft. She took comfort from the fact that they were few, those misfits, misanthropes, technophobes, romantics, irrationalists of every kind. Yet they did warn her of an underlying rebellious lust for adventure, the hunter heritage of the entire race. And . . . young, blond, tall, broad-shouldered, totally male, how beautiful the speaker was!

Omar's retort called her back. "That's unfair. Once you were more open-minded."

"Or I knew less," she said.

"Or Terra Central hadn't become your own center."

His bitterness bit her. "Are you that angry, Omar?"

He was instantly contrite. "I'm sorry. I didn't mean—" They sat silent for a number of heartbeats before he finished: "It seems, after all these years, we can still hurt one another."

*And the years will not return.* "Yes, I have changed," she said. "You too, no doubt, but I more." *Sometimes, lying awake at night, I miss the girl I was. Less her heedless health, dizzying joyfulness, even the quick sharp sorrows, than her dreams that knew no bounds.*

"Well, I'll listen to you, dear," she went on. "Then will you listen to me? While we can . . . Though I'd rather we talked about what's happened to us, like old friends come back together at last."

*And for the last time,* she foreknew.

## 2

Laurinda Ashcroft did not much revise her global braodcast later that day. It was one among several by well-known interfaces, intended over a period of years to make the danger clear and explain Terra Central's plan for coping. She had prepared most of it beforehand, the usual visuals plus occasional virtuals to invoke every sense.

Watching, you saw Earth revolve around the sun. You saw her orbit drawn in three dimensions, a golden track against blackness and the stars. You saw how she, her moon, and her sister globes interplayed a dance through billions of years, wherein gravitation called the measures, subtly but inexorably. You saw the slow cycle of changeable eccentricity and obliquity, how it set the patterns of lightfall across the planet and how she responded with her air, seas, clouds, rains, snow, and ice.

Since the Arctic Ocean became landlocked, the glaciers had come and gone and come again. In the great winters, northern Europe, half of North America, and huge tracts elsewhere lay under ice whose cliffs reared as high as two kilometers; drowned lands rose anew as sea level dropped a hundred meters; forests withered and died while south of them marshlands came into being and new forests overran the savannahs. Yes, life adapted. If some species suffered, others flourished. But this was on a millennial timescale, scant help to humans and their works.

The next glaciation was overdue. They had unwittingly delayed its beginnings with their emission of greenhouse gases. Now that was past, together with the overpopulation that brought it about, and in any event would not have sufficed. Now more snow fell in winter than melted in summer. Meter by meter, faster each year, the glaciers crept down from the Pole and the mountains.

"You have surely heard what we must do, and soon, before it is too late. Thicken the greenhouse. Thin the clouds. Darken the snows. Make Earth keep more of the sun's warmth than she can unaided. But perhaps you don't yet know the magnitude of this, the number of the centuries, or the delicacy and exactness underneath the enormous forces we will call on. Let me show you a little."

Again, visuals and virtuals. Carbon black strewn over the Arctic, tonne after colloidal tonne, repeated year after year as the layer washes away or sinks from sight. Immense electric discharges high aloft, to force rainfalls so that less light is cast back into space. Mats of brown algal weed carpeting the seas by millions of square kilometers; the care and feeding of these living artifacts. Underwater detonations to break up beds of methane hydrate and release the gas into the atmosphere. Forests set afire and afterward only grasses allowed, for they store less carbon than trees do. Holes drilled down into the very mantle of the planet; nuclear explosions to goad volcanoes into spewing forth carbon dioxide and water vapor more copiously than fossil fuels ever did. The new industries required, their claim on resources, their constructs and monitors everywhere.

"Yes, this will be an Earth very different from the Earth we thought we had restored for ourselves." Laurinda leaned forward, as if each person watching sat before her in the flesh. "But it will be far less changed than the Ice Age would change it. Our world will still be green, rich, kindly, from rim to rim of the Polar oceans. We will keep many of our woodlands, open waters, pure snowpeaks. And on the new prairies, what wildflowers will bloom, what herds will graze!"

She gave them the images, the sounds, the sense of wind and fragrances, simulated but as vivid as reality. *Idealized, yes. But not dishonest. We can have such places.*

"Please bear in mind, this will not happen at once. The work must go slowly, piecemeal, in pace with the astronomical cycle, constantly observed and measured, constantly adjusted to hold the giants of climate and weather under control. It will take thousands of years. Then finally, as Earth tilts back sunward, it will be undone, just as gradually and carefully. Most of us will notice little of it in our lifetimes. To our children and children's children, hundreds of generations, it will be natural, a part of their universe like the moon and stars."

"*That's the worst,*" Omar said. "*To them Terra Central will be what God was to their ancestors. Oh, I don't suppose they'll worship it. But they'll know how utterly dependent on it they are. And meanwhile it will be doing what God never did, evolve itself till it's beyond all human comprehension. What then, Laurinda?*"

Earlier, she had not meant to give his viewpoint as

much voice as she now did. However, this might actually be the wisest course. He and his fellows were making their protests widely known. By taking them seriously, she, a designated speaker for the artificial intelligence, could perhaps better show why they were wrong.

"Doubtless most of you have heard that certain people think this whole concept is mistaken." She left out Omar's *Disastrously mistaken. The more so because it's millennially slow and all-pervading.* She smiled. "They are not fools. They have studied the situation and done scientific analyses. Let me discuss their position as I see it. They are right when they say there is an easier, cheaper, and far less disruptive way to stop the Ice."

Robots in space. Asteroids mined, the stuff of them refined, nanotechnic assemblers forming titanic mirrors to precisions of micrometers, the judicious orbiting of these—no simple task, but well within present-day capabilities. Governed by mathematics and monitors less complex than in the rival scheme, the mirrors' shine added sunlight onto Earth at the times, places, and intensities needed. The glaciers retreat, climates stabilize, the system stands guard through the necessary era and stands in reserve forever after.

"It would take away the night skies we've regained. We would not see many stars, for there would be no full darkness. But simulacra are plentiful; or you can enjoy a holiday in space; and otherwise our world remains much the same.

"Why, then, does Terra Central warn against this?"

Again the bright, cold animated diagrams, but expanded first to a galactic scale, then contracted to Sol's near neighborhood, then down to molecules and force fields.

Space is not empty. Look at the Milky Way on a clear night and you will see bays in its river that are clouds of dust. The dust in such nebulas as Orion's is luminous from the light of new-born stars, and more are condensing out of it. Hydrogen and Helium, the primordial elements, far outmass these quantities of solid material, which are nevertheless colossal. Nowhere do the gas and motes of the interstellar medium reach a density equal to what would count as a hard vacuum on Earth; but taken together, through sevenfold billion cubic light-years, they dominate the visible universe.

Nor are they spread evenly. In some regions they occur more thinly or thickly than elsewhere. Sometimes a knot in the medium grows tight enough to collapse in on itself, and stars and planets form.

Sometimes, swinging around the galactic core on its two hundred million–year path, Sol encounters a dense cloud.

The one immediately ahead was nothing extraordinary. It would never engender worlds. It was merely a few times more compact than the local average and merely a few light-years in extent. Early astronomers had caught no definite sight of it. Even after they were using spaceborne instruments, they were not sure.

"Our interstellar outposts have the baselines to map this shoal with certainty. They have sent us their findings. In about nine thousand years, Sol will enter the region. Yes, it will only transect. A hundred thousand years later, it will be back in clear space. But a hundred thousand years is a long time for living creatures."

The contact presses on Sol's wind and magnetic field until the heliosphere and its bow wave, the hydrogen wall, are inside the orbit of Saturn. With the protection they give thus lessened, Earth takes a sleet of cosmic rays, background count tripled or quadrupled. Oh, life has survived comparable events in the past, but species, genera, whole orders died, ecologies to which they had been vital avalanched into ruin, mass extinctions followed. And, in the depths of this encounter, enough hydrogen atoms could reach Earth to deplete her oxygen, enough dust to fill her stratosphere with ice particles and bring on a world of winter like none before.

"Nine thousand years, our well-wishing opponents say. Ample time to make ready. Meanwhile, why should we lock ourselves into a program that will transform our civilization?

"People of Earth, through me and my colleagues Terra Central tells you that defense against the nebula calls for resources we dare not spend on anything less."

Monstrous constructions, thousands of them, in orbits that only machine intelligence can maintain—powered by thermonuclear reactions or often by the mutual destruction of matter and antimatter—and first the antimatter must be manufactured by megatonnes—generating forces to ionize alien atoms and whirl the plasmas away—a citadel around the entire globe, waging a war that lasts a tenth of a million years.

"Sun-mirrors to hold back the glaciers in the near future won't be compatible with this. Their advocates admit it, but say that come the time, we can make adjustments. Perhaps they are right. What they do not say is whether or not the mirrors will tie up too much material and effort. We'll have to conduct a very thorough survey of the Solar System before we know. Meanwhile, every year we delay starting to take action, the Ice advances farther and becomes harder to fight.

"But we, people of Earth, we now alive, who must make the decision that all our descendants must live with or die by—we should think beyond the engineering requirements. Let's ask ourselves a simple and terrible question. *In the course of nine thousand years, what can happen?*"

And she gave them history to show it was unforeseeable.

The Neolithic Revolution tamed wildernesses, fed
suddenly large populations, founded the earliest towns,
built the earliest smithies—and turned free hunters
into peasant masses with god-kings above them.

Scarcely were the Pharaohs of Egypt laid to their eternal rest than thieves plundered the tombs. When rail-
roads later ran through what had been their domains, for
a while the steam engines were stocked with mummies.

The Persian Empire fell into internecine war, then
fell to Alexander, whose own empire did not outlast his
untimely death. What followed was a prolonged blood-
bath.

Within four centuries of Jesus' entry into Jerusalem,
Christians were killing heretic Christians.

The peace and refinement of Heian Japan gave way
to incessant struggle between clans and war lords. In
China, dynasty after dynasty claimed the Mandate of
Heaven and eventually, bloodily, lost it.

The Mongols galloped from end to end of Asia, deep
into Europe, until their Khan reigned over half a continent. In a few generations that sovereignty crumbled.
Nonetheless a remnant of it turned the nascent democracy of Russia into the Tsardom, and another remnant
bore Islam to India.

The mighty Aztec and Inca realms broke before a
handful of Spanish invaders. The wealth that flowed
thence into Europe energized the trading nations of the
North but rotted Spain itself, whose long-term legacy
became one of tyranny and corruption.

From the "Liberty, Equality, Fraternity" of the French
Revolution sprang Napoleon. From the idealism of Sun
Yat-sen sprang Chiang Kai-shek and Mao Zedong.

No one in power understood what such modern weapons as the machine gun portended, nor was able to end the stalemate they brought before it had destroyed four empires, lives in the tens of millions, and the spiritual foundations of Western civilization. A greater war ensued, and then a twilight struggle for half a century more, while on its fringes countries newly established went at each other's throats.

In an age when science was reaching from the innermost atom to the outermost cosmos and scientific technology was transfiguring the human condition, ancient superstitions ran rampant, everything from astrology to witchcraft. What slowly overcame them was neither reason nor the major faiths but those lesser, often despised sects that had never compromised their creeds. Then slowly their own dominance eroded.

Instead of making governments almighty, global communications speeded the effective breakup of societies into self-determining coalitions of all kinds, ethnic, economic, religious, professional, cultural, even sexual.

Environmentalist crusaders preached, official agencies strove, but what rehabilitated an Earth devastated by overpopulation and overexploitation was a new set of technologies and the economic incentives and disincentives they brought about.

"There are no final answers, not while humans remain human. Nine thousand years is further ahead than our most ancient written records go back. What changes, what violences, what revolutions will they see? Above all, what revolutions of the spirit? We do not know.

"For the sake of our unborn and the sake of life itself on Earth, let us accept a few small sacrifices and make an irrevocable commitment *now* to the security of our planet—while we can do it, while we can choose to do it. Our descendants will bless us. Whatever they do, whatever they become, surely they will bless us. But already we, in this our mortal day, will have blessed ourselves."

# 3

Afterward Laurinda went topside for a walk. She needed motion and aloneness. In the house she felt too connected.

Evening light streamed low, nearly level. It seemed to fill grass and leaves with gold. A flight of nestbound rooks passed across the sky. Their calls drifted faintly down to her. A breeze cooled the air like a whisper from oncoming night.

Striding, she felt tension and anxiety drain away and peace flow out of the ground. It was as if her England thanked her.

The old church rose ahead. The machines that removed the deserted city had kept this relic, restored it, and maintained it. She spied an unobtrusive guardian robot—scarcely needed, as rare as visitors were. Another tended the graveyard. The names on the headstones were weathered into oblivion, yet somehow the headstones remembered.

So did the church she entered. A window above the doors made its own sunset. Elsewhere the stained glass glowed more softly, angels and saints under a ceiling that arched toward heaven. She could just make out Christ crucified above the altar. Not for the first time, she wondered how the archeologists and the machines—ultimately, Terra Central, in whose database lay all surviving records—decided what to model the emblem on; for the Puritans must have destroyed the original. Or had they? Sometime she should ask. The thought dropped from her. She sat down in a pew and listened to silence. She imagined ghosts gathered around, worshipful and humble, in the deepening dusk.

When she left, only a westward purple remained of the daylight. Soon that too was gone. Now and then she had to glance at the attendant on her wrist, which she had ordered to point the way back. Stars twinkled forth, one by one, more and more. Seen through this slightly misty air they were not as bright or as many as they might have been. Just the same, after a while their multitude and the sense of their remoteness came upon her. Which of those that she could see had intelligences reached by now? She wasn't sure. News from the explorers came in so slowly. Nor did she follow it very closely, being more concerned with Earth. Probably the explorers were still in Sol's purlieus. Nevertheless, those machines, traveling close to the speed of light, multiplying themselves wherever they found raw material and sending their offspring onward—in one or two million years the machines would have ranged over the whole galaxy.

Laurinda shivered. Once the vision had been glamorous and glorious. Tonight she began to ache, and recalled that she had eaten hardly anything all day. Yes, she was growing old.

Having descended to her house, she sought the part that was her own, not a workspace or entertainment and communication center or personal clinic but a small refuge for dreams. Virtuals weren't enough; she wanted reality, which whim could not alter. Wainscot made a background for framed pictures of ancient scenes and shelves of ancient books; the music she played was baroque; a copper kettle gave off steam, and soon her tea was ready and soon thereafter her supper, indistinguishable from one that might have been set forth for Jane Austen.

She didn't command the servitor to simulate a human retainer, nor instigate a search for a friend somewhere on the planet who would feel like conversing with her. She thought she wished only for quiet, a bit of reading, and then bed.

When a voice like her mother's contralto spoke to her, she realized that Terra Central had detected otherwise.

"May I interrupt? I would like to say you did wonderfully well. Public reaction has on the whole been positive and enthusiastic."

"Good," Laurinda said. "But I was just a single speaker. We need more."

Her mind went on: *The effort you are mobilizing moves softly but is huge. And what if it fails, if the vote does go against your urging? What might you then call upon?*

*And why do I think of you as a person?*

*Because you are. Not human; however, an awareness . . . a soul?*

"You were eloquent," said Terra Central, "and with an insight beyond mine."

Startlement answered, "How?" *What am I, that you are mindful of me?*

"Shall I explain tonight, or would you rather wait till you have rested?"

Terra Central was always considerate of her interfaces. Almost always, she guessed rightly. Laurinda's heart leaped. "Please, now."

The voice paused before continuing—to calm her a little? "I am dedicated to the well-being of life on Earth. No change I make in myself will change that. Your race is the sentient part of life. But I, as I am, cannot fully understand it.

"Texts, relics, perceptions, talks, are not the same as direct experience. I can follow the thoughts—even a shadow of the emotions—of gentle, rational humans such as you. But, I have not the capability, the empathy if you will, to interpret why others do what they do or why your history as a whole has followed the courses it did."

"Who, who does?" Laurinda stammered.

"It appears to me that your race is mad—not you, dear, nor most people by themselves, but your race— torn between instinct and intellect, the animal and something beyond the animal. Is this a misinterpretation? If not, then most likely, without guidance, humankind will put an end to itself long before the cosmos would. I cannot as I am understanding it well enough to know, or to provide that guidance.

"Help me, Laurinda."

"How?" she asked, atremble, wondering what further she could do in what years were left to her.

"Do not die. When your body is worn out, let me upload your mind and memories."

Cold struck through. "No! No. I've . . . thought about it, of course, but everything I've seen, everything I've heard—I don't want to be a robot."

"I know. But would you become one with me?

"A kind of Nirvana, yes, you no longer a uniqueness but an enrichment of the whole. Yet, you'll be there for millions of years or more, and, as need may be, I can resurrect you in emulation as you were.

"It's an offer I can only make to a few. This is a newly created capability, and my capacity for it is limited thus

far. Later—But I would like to take you, Laurinda, before you are gone forever.

"Think about it. Remember, though, your last hour
for choosing is not so very far away."

## VI

Seventeen hundred years later, a thing occurred that lived in people's memories for generations, until lifeways changed too much for them to make sense of it.

In those days communities, fellowships, nations, and ethnoi all had their own ways of observing New Century's Eve. In Tahalla it climaxed a month of ceremonies and celebrations. Some of these equalled Creation Day or Remembrance in solemnity, others rivaled Fire Night or the Festival for Children in joyousness. The quinquennial Darvic Games now took on an even greater importance; the glory that winning players brought to their clans would heighten the standing of every member and the influence of every captain for the next decade or more.

The opening procession moved grandiosely down Covenant Boulevard. Sunlight out of a hard blue sky flared off metal and seemed to set banners afire. Folk stood ten deep on either side. One did not sit at home and merely watch an occasion like this. One came, partook, joined in the hymns and the cheers, saw high-born and heroes pass by in the living flesh, felt the surge and throb of exultation, and needed no psychotrope for the spirit to soar. Most had arrived in groups, wearing the special garb of guild or society, but the groups had mingled randomly. The white gowns and red sashes of ed-

ucators might be wedged between the purple-and-gold
tunics of Magnificos and the scarlet cloaks and plumed
headdresses of Torchmen, or some Falcons in close-
fitting blue and gray cluster by some green-clad physicians. Only the philosophers kept individually apart, a
scattering of hooded gray robes trimmed with iridescent
flickercloth. As was their traditional right, the Terpsi-
choreans cavorted in front of everybody, on the street
itself, limbs, long hair, and filmy garments flying. The
morning was already hot, but nobody heeded. It baked
fragrances from the pavement.

Behind reared the many-hued walls, shimmering colonnades, and jewel-faceted cupolas of central Roumek.
Everything was cleaned and polished; often intricate
patterns of mosaic or sculpture had been added; but no
façade changed appearance except as shadows shifted
with the sun. Owners vied to produce astonishing effects
only at the Festival of Illusions. The Games were different, an occasion religious as well as secular.

Trumpets rang, sonors pealed and thundered, tuned
fountains and the Singing Tower blent their own music
in. Helmets and cuirasses agleam, lances and lasers held
high, a squad of Honorables went in advance, riding
white elks whose antlers had been gilded. Hierophants,
one from every hinterland in Tahalla, followed on foot,
wearing their canonicals and bearing their symbols according to their orders: of God the Dreamer of the Universe, God the Mother, God the Summoner (black
cassock, impaled skull), God the Lover (rainbow hues
and wreathed staff). After them glided the car of the
Holy Interpreter. Robotic agents attended his sumptu-
ously canopied throne and comforted him in his opalescent vestments with fans from which streamed cool
breezes. Another detachment of Honorables rode behind.

Then came the Regnant and First Consort. Their thrones were on a dais at the center of a great moving stage, from whose corners undulated the shapes of a golden dragon, a scarlet flame, a blue whirlwind, and a flowering vine. On the Regnant's left sat the heir apparent, on the Consort's right the Chief Enactor. Benched below were the Council. Senior guardsmen stood along the sides, tossing tokens of diamond and ruby into the crowd. The garb and accoutrements of all these dazzled every beholder.

A dozen men who stood at the front wore simply the insignia of the clans of which they were captains, together with emblems of whatever societies they might belong to—except for the one at the center, from whose shoulders hung the Cloak of Darva and in whose hand rested the Staff of Supremacy. Yet, gazes followed them more than any others: for these were the appointed stewards of the Games.

Magnates of the city, commanders of lesser communities, and rural landkeepers rode after, most in open cars, some on horses of fanciful genetics, each attired in his or her finest. Behind them marched the players, in bands under the standards of whatever contest they were to enter but every individual proudly dressed in a tunic of the color pattern marking his or her clan. And the shouts burst over them like surf.

Mikel headed the auvade contingent, for his father Wei, captain of Clan Belov, was among the stewards. Of course, kinship disqualified Wei from judging that competition. However, Mikel would have scorned nepotism and needed none; already he had won Second Master status. He should have gone toward the sacred grounds afloat on happiness, awaiting fresh renown at the very least, hoping for triumph.

Rancor filled his mouth. He felt as if the hurrahs

around him and the blossoms thrown at his feet were mockery. His overriding thought was of how he might turn victory into revenge.

## 2

Almost seven decades older than his son—otherwise he and his lady had set a good example and contented themselves with virtual children—Wei Belov took the matter stonily. "It is a disappointment, yes," he said. "It is not a humiliation unless we let it be."

Nevertheless, Mikel raged. So did a number of young clansmen. They roiled about the manor, crying denunciations of Arkezhan Socorro and the Chief Enactor, then whistling in unison the sinister ancient Gun Song. They galloped or careened over the countryside, to the terror of innocent grazers. They flitted to Roumek and got into drunken brawls with any Socorros they happened upon. Finally, Wei broadcast an injunction. "This behavior disgraces us," he declared. "It shall cease at once. Whoever continues it will be publicly censured and barred from next year's Affirmation Day rites." The furore died down.

None but his lady knew how he himself felt, and perhaps not even she. A captain of Clan Belov bore his own troubles uncomplainingly, as befitted his dignity. Still, she and Mikel could guess. His silences at home, his solitary walks, and his withdrawal from most global intercommunication told them much.

The Regnant should have made him not simply a steward but Supreme Steward of these Games. While the five-year cycle of succession was not immutable, it was customary, and this time Belov's turn fell on New Century's Eve. Wei had served well at earlier Darvics. Moreover, in his youth he had won trophies for mountain-eering on the moon and dune skiing on Mars. He was president of the national wildlife commission, which often involved him in interethnic negotiations under the auspices of the Worldguide. Surely, he deserved to bring this additional honor to his clan.

Now, for many years Arkezhan, Captain Socorro, had been his enemy. Wei never found out quite why. He knew of no harm he had ever done to the man or the clan, nor could he discover any that might have happened unwittingly. But Arkezhan was forever backbiting him, insulting him to the very limits of propriety, and playing nasty little tricks on him. At last Wei shrugged it off as due to jealousy. Arkezhan's career had been less than brilliant.

Yet, he made himself a favorite of Mahu, Captain Rahman, who became Chief Enactor of the realm. And Mahu prevailed upon the Regnant to appoint Arkezhan Supreme Steward of the Games.

The unspoken rejection fell like a soot cloud over all Clan Belov, deepest upon the captain and his immediate kin. Arkezhan crowed. His sycophants spread rumors.

Thus, matters stood on the day of the auvade.

## 3

Although a sunshade had deployed its film above the stadium, the tiers were brilliant with the clothes and jewels of spectators. From the judgment booth high up, they resembled terraced flowerbeds. Talk made a ceaseless murmur and rustle, as if one somehow heard the faraway sea. Down on the great hexagon, the teams stood alert, each man a spot of color on a tile along a given side, facing their mates on the opposite side, blue for Sirius, gold for Altair, red for Betelgeuse.

Wei leaned close to the viewer before which he sat
and whispered an order, for he did not wish to draw
attention to himself. The instrument scanned, identified
its target, and lighted with the image of his son. He
commanded an enlargement to one square meter.
There was Mikel, panther-poised, every muscle clear to
see beneath the form-fitting azure, bone strong in the
amber face, a defiant cockade in the headband confining
the raven's-wing hair—a Belov to the last chromosome.
His role was Comet; the insigne shone argent across his
breast. If only the boy were less tense, his look less grim.
Even more than strength and agility, a player needed
wits.

A voice brought Wei's glance around. Arkezhan Socorro had strolled over to his chair. "Ah," said the Supreme Steward, "you are anxious about your offspring,
I see."

With an effort, Wei remained seated. To be looked
down at like this was detestable, but to rise would show
irritation. And that would mean loss of dignity, especially here in the Presence. "I am interested, naturally,"
he answered as softly as he could. "Not anxious. He is
a capable athlete."

He slightly emphasized the pronoun. Arkezhan's son
took no part in sports and was rather notoriously un-
graceful in both social and ceremonial dancing.

Arkezhan concealed whatever he felt. "That will be
for impartial stewards to determine." He nodded at the
three of them, Ibram Ahmad, Jon Mitsui, and Malena
Mogale, where they sat ready at their own viewers. They
sensed hostility in the air and looked uncomfortable.

"The fairmindedness of my lords and my lady is beyond question," Wei said, "unlike some."

It was an awkward rejoinder. He had never been good

at such exchanges. Arkezhan smirked. He shook his jowly head and wagged a finger the barest bit. "Yes, I have to accept their assurance that you will not abuse your privilege today."

The three had in fact been very kind when they invited Wei, an old friend, to share the booth and its superb observation facilities. Maybe now, too late, they realized that Arkezhan was making it a mistake. Wei bit the inside of his lip. He would not embarrass them.

"You have my thanks for agreeing, sir," he said more loudly. Swinging his chair around, he saluted the Regnant. "And all gratitude always to his gracious Radiance." The formula tasted foul in his mouth.

Had he known beforehand that the Regnant would attend, he would probably have declined the invitation. Some heads of state in the past had observed a few contests, but usually this one appeared just at the opening of the Games. For that matter, the Supreme Steward did not necessarily oversee any particular event in person, though every judgment booth kept a seat and viewer for him. Who had persuaded these two to be here, and how and why?

Maybe, they were honestly interested. Auvade had a great many devotees, not only throughout Tahalla but around all Earth and among what humans still lived elsewhere in the Solar System; probably millions were watching today.

Wei couldn't tell. The Regnant sat impassive on the throne extruded for him, above and behind the Supreme Steward's chair. Scarcely a fold of his robe and chasuble or plume of his headdress stirred.

Jon broke a lengthening silence. "With reverence, your Radiance, with respect, my lord, the time draws nigh."

"Indeed," Arkezhan said. "I regret, my lord Wei, we

cannot hear your doubtless fascinating conversation. I
am sure you would have told us much about the wonders
of young—Niho? No, I beg your pardon, the name is
Mikel, am I correct? Instead, we must witness them ourselves." He bowed to the Regnant. "Have I the permis-
sion of the Presence to take my place?"

A hand lifted and fell again. Arkezhan sat down. "Let
the honors begin," he said. Amplified, the words boomed
forth.

Trumpets resounded. Spectators roared. The diffused
blur in the sunshade became a gigantic view of the
board.

For a moment there was motionlessness. Each team
had had its conferences, planning strategy and tactics
to minimize its losses and maximize those of the others,
until the last survivors belonged only to it; but now the
reality was upon them.

Then a Sirian Star ran one tile forward along the
straight line permitted him and stopped. A Planet came
diagonally from either side to stand in front; two Moons
made their three zigzags to take flanking positions, and
two Meteors overleaped—passed across tiles occupied
by a friendly player—to threaten Altair on the right and
Betelgeuse on the left. The Comets stayed in reserve.
This maneuver was classic, creating a strong defensive
formation. The Sirians across from them advanced aggressively, though not far since they did not know who
their opponents would be.

Those had begun somewhat similarly. An Altairian
Star dashed ahead to the middle of the board and
halted. A Betelgeusean Planet took the bait and slanted
onto the same tile. They saluted one another. The Star
advanced. The Planet sought to take the attack on his
hip and throw his opponent, who would automatically
lose if he crossed an edge of this tile. But the latter

shifted direction, turned on one heel, got his other ankle behind the former's, and pushed. The Planet caught the Star's arm. Both lurched, neither went down. They broke apart, considered the situation, and sidled back in again. Abruptly the Planet went down onto the resilient surface, the Star on top, pinning him. They separated, rose, and bowed. The Planet retired from the game. Immediately, a Sirian Moon arrived. Given the advantage of freshness, he took the position.

Bouts had been erupting elsewhere. It was no melee. A player looked at the overall scene displayed overhead, decided as best he could what move might best help his team, and tried to make it and win it.

"What, does Comet Mikel still dawdle?" said Arkezhan. "Does he wait for rivals to exhaust each other?" He clicked his tongue. "It is no real service, it certainly gives no glory, although it may make his individual performance seem better than otherwise."

"He plans—" Wei Belov broke off. He should no longer speak in this place.

After a few more minutes Mikel did advance, choosing two tiles sideways and one forward, then one oppositely sideways and two forward, out of the moves allowed him. It brought him to an Altairian Moon. They engaged. He prevailed. The Moon withdrew.

Mikel paused, peering upward. He was about to advance on a Betelgeusean Comet—at least, that seemed to be his optimum tactic—when a Betelgeusean Meteor took him by surprise. If they reached an edge of the board, Meteors could cross back to the opposite edge and proceed from there, as if the two sides were contiguous. However, they must move in straight lines and, unlike Stars, cross no more than six tiles before stopping, unless and until they were victorious at their end point.

Mikel barely gave him courtesy. They grappled ungracefully. The Meteor fell, though merely onto his rear. Mikel leaped and forced his shoulders to the ground. He conceded and left. By then, of course, the situation elsewhere had changed and Mikel's earlier idea was of no use.

"Poor, poor form," said Arkezhan. "Score his team down."

"My lord," protested Ibram, "the action was not very esthetic, but I found no real fault."

"Nor I," added Malena. Jon could say nothing, his attention having been on others.

"Did you not observe how he butted with his arms and fumbled with his hands?" Arkezhan replied. "Score his team down, I say. Three points." Each counted as a man lost, which might force the Sirians out of the game early, and the record would show this was due to Mikel Belov.

"One at most, my lord," Malena argued. "Few actions are ever perfectly executed."

"Three."

Nobody refused. Arkezhan was Supreme Steward, after all; and the designated stewards had plenty else to grip their attention; and markdowns, frequent enough in any closely refereed contest, canceled each other by apportionment among the two rival groups.

Wei's mouth drew tight.

The auvade went on. The spectators yelled, waved kerchiefs and flags, pranced on their benches when someone's idol was victorious.

"Behold what an opportunity our Mikel Belov missed," said Arkezhan after some minutes. "If he had taken that Altairian Planet, a Betelgeusean Comet would have been open to attack by an Altairian Star. However that encounter came out, there would have been one less survivor for the Sirians to meet."

"Yes," admitted Ibram. He studied the skyscene. "Easy for us to see. But who in the midst of an engagement can survey it all?"

"Competent players can, to a considerable extent. Of course, possibly our brave little Comet did not choose to meet the Planet, who does appear quite formidable."

Malena scowled into her viewer. "My lord, you seem determined to pursue this man," she said. "We have others to watch as well."

"Of course. I would not criticize your decisions, my lady and my lords. But you must agree that certain players require more zealous monitoring than most. For the good of the game."

"My lord, I do not feel that Mikel Belov is among them."

Arkezhan shrugged. "Well, you may be right, my lady. You are old acquaintance with his family, are you not? Very close old acquaintance."

Malena stiffened.

"If you please, my lord," said Jon, ice in his voice.

Arkezhan raised his palms. "Oh, no, no! I would never imply, nor imagine for an instant, that my lady or either of my lords would heed any offer that any player's father may have made."

Wei snapped after air. The Regnant sat expressionless. The stewards could not respond, for the game was becoming ever more rapid and complex.

Suddenly Arkezhan raised his eyes from his own viewer and cried, "A foul, a foul!"

"What?" The stewards' heads jerked about toward him.

"Did you miss it? When Mikel Belov met that Altairian Moon just now, he grabbed after the man's groin."

Wei's knuckles whitened on the arms of his chair.

Malena forgot civility. "He did not."

"Were you watching him, my lady?" Arkezhan replied. "You have the entire board to follow. I choose to focus on where my suspicions lie."

Wei half rose. Ibram said hastily, "My lord the Supreme Steward probably missaw, as can happen to anyone. We will replay the encounter in slow motion if he insists."

Arkezhan smiled. "No need, my lord. I will accept your judgment. Perhaps I was mistaken. Perhaps in the excitement I confused a tendency with an intent."

Wei got to his feet. His face was blanched. "Sir," he said word by word, "I trust that that remark was inadvertent and you will retract it and apologize."

The stewards kept their gazes on the viewers, scanning to and fro, as duty required; but Malena blurted, "Your Radiance has heard—" She broke off, appalled at herself.

The Regnant sat unstirring.

Arkezhan smiled. "Why, I meant no harm, my lord, no basic fault to find. We are what we are. That boy has evidently chosen to do little or nothing about the characteristics he has inherited from, say, his mother."

Wei stepped forward. He doubled his fist and struck. Arkezhan staggered back. The stewards gasped. As if it too had seen, the crowd howled.

Arkezhan recovered his stance. Blood trickled from his nose. He grinned.

## 4

The lands for which Clan Belov was responsible lay near the northern border of Tahalla. Beyond it continued the same Arabiyah, hills and valleys where the wind sent waves across tall grass, tossed fronds and soughed through leaves, where streams flowed into shining lakes, where great herds and their predators bounded and a flying flock often cast a shadow like a cloud's—but the folk of Zayan had ways very different from the ways of Tahalla. So did all folk everywhere on Earth, and from each other.

Wei set his car down at the foot of a hill and climbed to the top. As he mounted he saw more and more widely. In the distance giraffes mingled with lyrehorns and a few cheirosaurs, ignoring a pride of lions stretched sleepy on a ridge. Impulsively, meaninglessly, he waved at them. Though the reintroduction of rare species, the rebirthing of many that had gone extinct, and creation of others that never evolved happened before his lifetime, he had experienced it so often in virtuality that he felt as if he had been there, helping—as if he had even played some part, however humanly insignificant, in staving off the Ice. It gave depth and passion to the day-by-day ecological management that was his main reality occupation.

He had found a lonely place. An unobtrusive upthrust on the western horizon was the dome of a food production center, purely robotic. Smoke rose, thin and quickly scattered, from a swale kilometers off, an excursionist campfire, but that belonged, recalling a Stone-Age his race had forgotten but his genes had not.

His muscles tautened, flexed, and tautened again, bearing him upward against gravity. Sunlight fell warm on his face, air passed warm through his nostrils. Earth bore no medicine for shame and grief, and he would not smother them together with his honor in drugs, but Earth itself was a balm.

He had chosen this hill because a eucalyptus grove stood on the crest, a screen across heaven. Should a survey-satellite chance to pass overhead, he didn't want it making any record of these next moments. The shade fell cool and dappled, pungencies swirled, leaves seemed to whisper his farewells for him.

He had said none when he left home today, only that he wanted to get away for a while. "I understand," his lady answered. He suspected that she understood all too well, and her calm was her last gift.

*I'm sorry, Lissa, Mikel,* he thought. *There is no better way to regain our pride. Is there? May you live gladly.*

He drew his pistol. The single round in it was not a stun cartridge. Revival would be out of the question.

Carefully, he brought the muzzle to his temple. *A cold kiss,* he thought. Then: *Don't linger.*

The shot crashed. A vulture high overhead started down in long, slow spirals.


# 5


Sesil Hance occupied a house on the outskirts of Roumek, an ornate thing of columned pillars and slender turrets, intended for a family larger than any nowadays but easily and variably adaptable for entertaining. Windows threw a soft glow into the night. Music played low, a piece the house had lately composed. From thirty meters away, its nearest neighbor joined in. Otherwise, the street lay quiet, empty except for a gardener robot at work in the flower strips.

The main door knew Mikel Belov and retracted for him. He stepped into an anteroom of mahogany panels, nacre ceiling, and live carpet. Two figures appeared in full-size holography, an older man and woman. Propriety forbade a clan maiden to receive male visitors alone. Sesil's parents preferred their rural estate. They had

had these virtuals of themselves prepared for her, to speak and act as they would and record whatever the sensors observed. She had told him they trusted her and never retrieved the data. It was simply a matter of maintaining repute.

He saluted. "Greeting, Mikel Belov," said the likeness of Yusuf Hance formally, and, equally formally, "Be welcome" the likeness of Fiora Hance.

"I thank you, my lord and lady," he replied.

Sesil came through an inner archway. A black gown over which star-points twinkled clung to her. She stopped. A hand went to her mouth. "Oh," she breathed. Her eyes widened, as luminously dark as the fabric. "You. I hoped so much—Come, please come." To the images: "By your leave." She turned and led her visitor out, down a hall to a room where odors of jasmine drifted and colors played subtly through the walls. Though she turned back towards him, she made no move to join hands or to touch at all. "Please rest, my lord." She made a ragged gesture at a lounger. "May I summon refreshment?"

He kept his feet. "You have not called me lord for more than a year," he said. They had been close to betrothal. He stopped himself from adding "my lady."

Her glance dropped. How long the lashes were on that delicate countenance. "No. It's only—now—the tragedy befallen you—and now you will be Captain Belov."

"If they elect me. That must wait a while." Pain broke through. "Sesil, why haven't I heard from you?"

She gestured at the holo cabinet. It came alight with the simulacra of her parents. She had seldom done that before—no impoliteness, for the realities would have left the young couple to themselves. "Did she want help?" Mikel repeated his question.

"You know why, my lord," pseudo-Yusuf told him.

Sesil's fingers twisted together. "I, I would have," she stammered, "I wanted to, I wanted to, but—" She could not go on.

He finished for her. "But my father had done a deed of violence upon a fellow officer, and in the very Presence. His whole clan was in dishonor."

"That was so unjust!" she cried.

Mikel addressed the images. "You"—he meant the realities—"would not thereafter deal with a Belov."

Yusuf's voice answered slowly: "We could not very well, could we?"

"Be honest, dear," said Fiora's. Analogue tears glimmered. "We dared not."

*Yes,* Mikel thought, *too many other Hances would feel you had tainted them also.* "I quite understand, my lord and lady," he said. "For my part, I had no wish to put you in a difficult position."

Sesil raised her head and squared her frail shoulders. "But your honor is made clean again," she said. The steadiness failed. "I hoped—I hoped—" She swallowed. "Yes, I wept for you, for him, but now—"

Mikel nodded. "Well, I might have come sooner." He did not patronize with an apology. "My mother and I have been busy."

"Of course." He barely heard Sesil. "And I, I didn't want to . . . break in. I waited. Now you are here." She half reached for him.

Yusuf's voice intervened. Her arms dropped. "With respect, my lord, that was a dreadful means of setting matters right. He could have gone into exile."

Mikel's fists clenched at his sides. "And drag through life among aliens, a friendless, helpless outsider?"

"Communication—telepresence—"

"That would have made it worse. We would have lived

with the daily knowledge of his condition. No, my father made what he believed was a clean and final ending."

Pseudo-Yusuf overlooked the rude interruption and replied mildly. "He has made total atonement. Thereby we can resume."

Fiora's voice: "We too will pay him honors, by name, at every Remembrance."

Mikel shook his head. "As you like, my lady, and thank you for your generosity. But this is not yet done with. I do not accept that my father owed any atonement." He looked back at Sesil. "I came to bid you goodbye."

She shuddered. "What?"

"My father acted under intolerable provocation. Witnesses agree. The Regnant surely recognized this. He should have spoken it forth, called my father fully justified, pardoned the breach of Radiant dignity, and reprimanded Arkezhan Socorro. He did not."

"What do you mean?" Sesil swallowed. "To do?"

"The Regnant shall proclaim the justification and the pardon, and lay the dishonor where it belongs," Mikel stated.

The face of Yusuf went expressionless. "How do you propose to accomplish this?" the voice murmured.

"I will have men with me, my lord. Let that suffice."

"More violence? No!" Sesil snatched after his hand. A fingernail scratched. She clung. "No, I beg you."

"Wish you to disgrace your clan afresh?" pleaded phantom Fiora.

"Of course not." The program in an ancient gun might have spoken as coldly as Mikel. "I have studied the historical database. Precedents exist."

"Buried," pseudo-Yusuf protested. "Essentially forgotten." It/he must have made a hurried search. "Yes, you can invoke things done in desperate times, during the Oceanic Rebellion and the turbulence afterward. But that was long ago."

"For generations they were the stuff of tales and ballads. The precedents they set have never been rescinded."

"Because no one afterward ever imagined—" The simulacrum did not continue.

"My lord and ladies, I have told you what I have told you in privacy, as a guest in your home," Mikel reminded.

Fiora's image winced. "That was needless to say."

"Yes, of course we will maintain confidentiality until you release us; and it is clear that debate would serve no purpose," added Yusuf's stark tone.

Sesil let go of Mikel. She took a backward step from him. "You . . . you've become a stranger. I didn't know you could dream of such a thing."

"I regret the necessity," he said.

"That you call it a necessity—oh, horrible—"

Mikel saluted. "Good evening, my lord, my ladies." He made his unescorted way back into the night.

# 6

The captain's mansion of Clan Socorro lay surrounded by a garden of delights that hid it from the surrounding estate. Thereby the dozen men who came toward it afoot over the meadowland were also covered against sight, unless someone spied them by chance. Then they would rouse curiosity, but scarcely alarm. Clad for outdoors, no emblems clearly visible, they looked like any group enjoying a few days in the open, whether as licensed hunters or just trekkers. It would be natural for them to draw near, admire the garden, and maybe hope for an invitation to see the house.

Olver took a biodetector from his pouch and squinted at it. "Two persons along the most direct path," he said.

Mikel nodded. "Something like that was to be expected," he replied redundantly. They were all tense. Sunlight glinted off sweat. The wind felt stronger and colder than it was, its rustle in the leaves ahead louder.

Nonetheless the band continued steadily. They had studied, planned, and rehearsed; and they were men of Clan Belov—young men, in whom old stories had come back to life.

A line of candle bamboo, coldly aglow, reared before them. "Go," said Mikel. He kept his voice quiet. Four deployed right, four left, to cover the flanks. Three followed him straight in through the hedge.

Beyond, in shifting light and shadows, serpentine trees swayed sinuously, iridescence shimmered on pearl bush, an oak spread majestic boughs, moonflowers went from phase to phase, the path wound through endless variety. Around almost every turn waited some surprise, a dancing sculpture, a pool of tinted mist, an arrangement of stones, a miniature antelope that poised in its beauty before it leaped out of view. Ten species of birds caroled in chorus. Fragrances drifted sweet, smoky, spicelike, sometimes slightly intoxicating or erotic or otherwise stimulating.

Where a bridge arched over a brook, a man and a woman stood, perhaps enjoying the place and one another. Their eyes widened in startlement as the invaders appeared. Pistols were already out. Before anyone could shout a warning, the woman crumpled. She would only be unconscious for an hour or so, but lying there in her raiment she was pathetically like a heap of rags.

The man, tall and powerful, had also dropped. It was

a lightning-swift deception. The shot at him had missed. He bounded back to his feet. More shots, fired in surprise, went wild. He sprang behind a weeping willow and thence into deeper reaches. A roar trailed after him: "Belov! I know you!"

Mikel's party traded glances. "I know him too," Olver said. "Dammas, Arkezhan's nephew. I've seen him run down horses and wrestle bulls."

"Ill luck," groaned Teng.

"Proceed the faster," Mikel ordered. "Vahi's squad may well take care of him."

The bridge thudded under their feet. The garden soon gave way to lawn. The house loomed ahead. A machine stopped work, uncertain what this meant. Several peacocks squawked and scattered. The companion detachments broke out into view. They converged from left and right, to join their fellows in the final headlong dash.

Up the ramp and across the portico they went. The main door grew suspicious and began to draw shut. Mikel had prepared for that. Nothing here was planned for serious defense, not after three centuries of the Great Peace. One of his pistols carried explosive rounds. An assembler in a cellar had secretly crafted them for him. He fired with precision. Impact crashed. Shock passed through to the embedded computer. The door halted half open. The raiders stormed inside.

Polished marble encompassed them. Fish swam below a transparent floor. A rampway swept upward. A few individuals, drawn by the noise, saw what was entering and fled. They were merely attendants, ceremonialists, entertainers, or the like. One stood fast, gray, weather-beaten, obviously a kinsman here on a visit. "Who the filth are you?" he exclaimed.

Vahi and Turkan closed in to seize his arms. "Where is Arkezhan Socorro?" demanded Mikel.

"Hoy-ah?" Now the man saw the small clan insignia on the newcomers' breasts. "Belovs! All of you! What is this outrage?"

"We require direct speech with Captain Arkezhan. We know he's at home. If we must ransack, there may well be trouble, ancestral treasures damaged, people hurt or even killed. For everybody's sake, tell us."

"He—he may be gone—"

Mikel sneered. "So you believe your noble captain forsakes his folk and their heritage in an hour of danger?"

Angry but shaken and bewildered, the man blurted, "Never! I, I saw him last . . . in the Winter Room."

"Likely enough," Teng said. "Doesn't he often flit to the high North?"

"Claims it inspires him," Olver growled. "To what foulness this time?"

The loyalty of his followers, their rage on his behalf and his father's, stirred Mikel's spirit anew. He had wondered earlier how many there were to whom clanship meant anything other than relationships and rituals. Now, he wondered how many more would have risen like these had he called on them. All?

Then it must be the same for the Socorros. He'd better exploit the advantage of surprise while he had it. "Come," he said. The men let their prisoner go and ran up the rampway at his heels. The house had been famous for generations; its layout was public knowledge.

Stillness brooded in long halls and spacious chambers. Mikel wondered fleetingly if the house ever called back to mind the days when life and noise filled it, when children had kept it busier than everything else put together. Aghast: *Children!* But surely, if any were present, they had immediately been taken out of harm's way.

A pair of men had armed themselves with wine bottles, the only weapons to hand. They stood forlornly brave in the last corridor. Two stun shots laid them out. The invaders burst into the room beyond.

The air was cool here, though the true cold lay in a simulacrum of an Arctic region where some polar cap had been preserved—glacier and snowfield, blue-shadowed white, and a black glimmer of sea between ice floes. The scene dwarfed Arkezhan. He stood before a multifunctional terminal, clutching a fur-lined robe to him. The cabinet was needlessly large, gold-inlaid ebony with a rock crystal desk surface. *You always were vainglorious,* Mikel thought. *If only I could spatter you against those screens like a swatted fly.*

Did Arkezhan tremble beneath his garment? His tone certainly quavered shrill: "What are you doing? Are you deranged? Is this some obscene prank? Get out! Go at once!"

"We will when we have completed our business with you," answered Mikel around the lump of hatred in his gullet.

"What business? Your own ruination? Are you aware—"

"Be still."

"No. You—peacebreaker—"

Mikel grabbed him by the shoulders and shook him till his teeth rattled. "Be still and listen." Arkezhan stared at the younger, stronger man and the grimness behind him. "Sit down. Over there." Mikel hustled him to a chair a few meters off.

The men posted themselves, alert, two of them at the terminal. Vahi began to monitor the house and its activities. Olver called up outside views to cover every direction. Now and then he magnified for a closer scan.

Mikel paced to and fro before the chair. Arkezhan

gripped its arms and perforce looked up. His features writhed.

The winter seemed to speak through Mikel. "You know full well why we are here. You deliberately provoked my father Wei, Captain Belov, to the point where his sole choice was to avenge his honor and the honor of his family."

Arkezhan rallied. "Nonsense. If he was so unreasonable as to take offense at a few remarks, he could have made complaint later. The dishonor sprang from his behavior, there before the *Regnant*."

"He would not repeat your vile words in a suit at law for the whole nation to hear."

*I exaggerate,* Mikel knew. *My father did lose control. But he was goaded beyond a proud man's endurance. And he was my father and the captain of my clan.*

"Well, he could have complained at once," Arkezhan said.

"The Regnant would have referred the matter to the Chief Enactor." *If the Regnant did not simply dismiss it on the spot. He must have heard what went on, and spoke no word.* "Thereupon you would have kissed Mahu Rahman's . . . hand . . . as usual, and suffered not so much as a reproof."

Arkezhan flushed and started to rise. "Now you impugn my honor." Mikel gestured and he sank back. "This is intolerable. I shall enter criminal charges against you and your gang."

Mikel shook his head. "No. You shall admit your own guilt directly to the Regnant. He will proclaim it, absolving my father of every blame."

Arkezhan gasped. "You dare—you, who have broken into my home, terrified and assaulted my people—"

"In view of the mitigating circumstances, and at your urgent request, the Regnant will publicly annul every offense of ours. He will emphasize that the honor of Clan Belov remains unstained."

"How can you imagine this?"

Mikel shrugged and grinned a bit. "I daresay the Chief Enactor will have prevailed on him. You see, if it does not come about, we will kill you."

Arkezhan gaped like one stunned.

"We will then make the truth known to the whole world," Mikel went on. "And then, of course, we will ourselves die—free. The story will live on."

"To the disgrace of your clan," Arkezhan said frantically.

"Oh, no. Do you suppose we haven't given it thought? Similar occurrences in the past came to be regarded as glorious. Our deaths will atone, as my father's did for a fault that was not even his. The Belovs will remember us in pride. Tahalla will. Tell me, though, how can Clan Socorro ever lose the infamy?"

Arkezhan sat mute.

Mikel halted his pacing. "You will properly serve your people, you, their captain, if you do what we ask," he said. "The Regnant will doubtless pardon your admitted wrongdoing. That should suffice."

*In his mind, he will certainly never pardon us. We must always be on guard against a sly vengeance. I will encourage every Belov household to keep arms and train in their use.*

"Think," Mikel said. "Do not be slow about it."

"Absolutely not," Olver called. "Look."

Mikel went over to the screens. Men were emerging from the garden. Olver enlarged the view. They straggled, unskilled, but they moved resolutely and they carried hunting weapons. A skyward scan showed two cars approaching.

"That Dammas," Olver opined. "A Socorro, but a

man. He's pulled together those who fled from the house, equipped them from the gamekeeper's lodge, and sent for help from other homes."

Mikel's followers reached for their lethally loaded guns. Some cursed. A sudden, strange detachment came over him. *Is this how soldiers felt in the old days?* he wondered. He turned back to his prisoner. "You can prevent a fight," he said. "Tell them to hold off."

"I—I do not know if I can—by now." Arkezhan got to his feet. His head lifted, his tone steadied somewhat. "Or if I should."

*No,* went Mikel's cold thought, *your captaincy would ever after be hollow, wouldn't it?*

"Maybe they'll only lay siege," Vahi said.

"Till the Regnancy hears, if it hasn't already, and sends reinforcement," Olver replied.

*If the Chief Enactor dares,* Mikel thought. *He is not popular with most of the clans. He must know the consequences will be unforeseeable. That was part of what we counted on. But in any case, we will have overwhelming strength against us.*

Arkezhan gained nerve. "Now that they are heartened, my folks will not tolerate what they realize is my humiliation," he said. "And they will, absolutely, have exact justice for my death. They have the same historical examples to cite that you do, and more clearly applicable. Yield, and perhaps I can negotiate safe conduct for you out of this trap you have closed on yourselves."

Mikel sighed. "That is impossible for us. Have you enough rudimentary sense of honor to understand? We will fight, and no one shall take any of us alive." He slid his killer pistol from the sheath. A harsh glee leaped. "Least of all you."

"No," proclaimed a new voice.

# 7

It came not from any throat or any instrument. Maybe the walls of the house reverberated with it, soft though it was. The men outside must have heard it too, for they stopped in their tracks.

The voice was a deep contralto, calm and implacable. "Desist." Abruptly, heatlessly, every weapon within a kilometer slumped into uselessness.

Down on the grass, men stood as if frozen, or sank to their knees. Three screamed and bolted back into the garden. The cars aloft stopped and hovered. Up in the Winter Room, Arkezhan sagged down again. Mikel's followers stared at their emptied hands or wildly around at the ice.

"You were about to go beyond a brawl or even a murder," said the voice. "You would have broken the Peace of the Covenant."

It was the Worldguide that spoke, Mikel knew. Amidst tumult, a tiny part of him wondered how much of its attention the central intelligence of the Solar System was giving to this occasion and this moment.

"Did you think your actions went unobserved?"

The machines, robots, planetary maintenance, the whole incomprehensibly vast meshwork of communications, computations, and information, Mikel realized. Yes, and satellites, and invisibly small flying sensors, everything in the service of humankind and of life everywhere, therefore its deeds and decisions unquestioningly—gladly—accepted by nearly every person alive.

"Your own laws, usages, and consciences preserved it thus far in this nation. Your own ceremonies, rituals, vyings for status, and pleasures took up your energies."

*What else was left for us?* cried the unborn rebel.

"But now that very tradition has led you to reignite the old violence. Unchecked, it would burn more fiercely from generation to generation, resentment, blind hate, feud, war, with unrest in many other societies. It must end at once."

The voice mildened the barest bit. "Take comfort. Yours is not the first country where the threat has arisen, nor will it likely be the last, for long times to come. Always the flame has been quietly damped. So it shall be here.

"The raiders shall go freely home. There shall be no penalty upon them, overt or covert, and their people may feel themselves vindicated if they so desire; but neither shall there be penalty for anyone else, or revenge—ever, in the lifetimes of you and your descendants.

"Go in peace. Abide in peace."

No words about enforcement were necessary.

The voice fell silent. Slowly, men looked into one another's eyes.

In a rush of horror, which was followed by relief and a kind of resignation, Mikel thought: *Now we know our future.*

# ∞ VII ∞

The day came when that which had been Christian Brannock asked for an ending.

He supposed it had happened before, and surely it would happen again, across spans of centuries and light-centuries. Not that he knew how many of him had come into being, copied and recopied. The memories of this one recorded only four such births. In each case, an intelligence had wanted to leave a place where a Brannock chanced to be. Generally, it had stopped there in the course of exploration farther into the galaxy, seeking a site auspicious for the founding of a new outpost of intelligence. The intelligence wanted helpers with various abilities, less of the body—a body could be designed and made for any special purpose—than of the mind, the spirit. Brannock's ranked high among the humanlike. Thus, he could hardly ever simply join the expedition. He was still needed where he was.

A new uploading gave a new Brannock, eager to go. Often the older Brannock watched the departure with something akin to wistfulness. However, the work he had been engaged in remained fascinating and challenging. Should it cease to be so, then he could shut himself down. Eventually, he would be reactivated, aroused, to a fresh undertaking or to a ship willing to carry him elsewhere.

"Old" and "new" had little meaning, though. Immediately after an uploading, the two information-patterns of his basic self were essentially identical. Afterward their destinies diverged, and different experiences wrought different changes in them. Any single line of such a many-branched descent could only guess at what had become of the others. If once in a great while chance brought two individuals together, they met as strangers.

Yet to all of them, "age" was meaningful. They existed not in short-lived, vulnerable flesh, but in enduring molecules and in data flows, complex energy exchanges, with no inevitable mortality. Nevertheless, time passed for them too. Being sentient, they felt it. At last it brought a certain weariness upon them.

This Brannock on this day flew above a planet far from Earth. Sol was invisible among its stars after dark. At the moment its sun stood small and dazzling in a greenish sky. Red-tinged clouds drifted on winds that a human could not have breathed and lived. Lakes glinted in the glare. Heat-shimmers danced over low hills and the growth upon them. Those mats, stalks, fluttering membranes, and spongy turrets were purple, ruddy, gold, in a thousand mingled shades. Now and then swarms of tiny creatures whirled aloft. Light shattered into sparks of color where it struck them.

To Brannock the world was beauty and marvel. It did not threaten him. Nor did raw rock or empty space; but here was life. That it was primitive hardly mattered, in a universe where life of any kind was so rare as to seem well-nigh a miracle. That it was altogether alien to Earth's made it a wellspring of knowledge, from which Intelligence Prime and, through its communications, intelligences across the known galaxy had been drinking for these past seven hundred years. The farthest off among them had not yet received the news; photons fly too slowly.

And Brannock had shared in the enterprise: helping establish the first base; helping build the industries necessary for its maintenance, enlargement, and evolution; helping explore, chart, study, discover. Often, his quests had been difficult, even precarious. Always they had been adventures.

The goal was nearly gained, the planet was nearly understood, what remained was an almost algorithmic research that did not require him. Intelligence Prime was turning its attention to other things. Once Brannock had meant to go unconscious when that time came, to wait for recruitment into some undertaking new and mysterious. But time itself had worn away the desire.

Because this would be his last journey, he took care to savor it. Instead of merely communicating his intent, he went in a material body, which he had chosen just for the purpose. It flew, through its sensors, he felt power coursing, control surfaces flexing, air slipping by like water by a swimmer; he heard and tasted its changeableness; he scanned over wide horizons or magnified perception to follow the least of living creatures kilometers below. The flight was his farewell to a phase of existence.

He passed above a seashore. Tides were weak, on this world without a moon, but wind raised surf and blew foam off wave crests. Microbes yellowed the water. An island hove in sight. He slanted down toward it. Eagerness lifted, though it was largely intellectual, maybe not unlike the feelings of an ancient mathematician as a theorem came together for him. Once upon a time Brannock's heart would have racketed, his blood pulsed, his muscles tensed, the breath gone quickly in and out. But he was a man then.

A young man, at that . . . once upon a time.

And a man of the West, not the East. Even when old, would he have looked forward to losing selfhood?

*Well,* he thought for an electronic instant, *I expected to lose it when I died, and suddenly I sidestepped that. This today won't actually erase me. It will—I don't know what it will be like. I'm not capable of knowing. Not as I now am.*

He landed, folded his wings, and advanced.

Before him loomed a—call it a huge, many-faceted jewel. Say that lightnings and rainbows moved over it, shone from it, made a dancing glory around it. Say that low domes and high pylons stood in attendance, while air and ground murmured with unseen energies. Brannock perceived more than this; the sensors of his body were more than human. Still, he knew that much was intangible to him, incomprehensible, force fields, quantum computations, actions far down in the foundations of reality.

He did notice changes since last he was here. They were no surprise. The reigning intelligence at this star was always changing itself. And it did not do so alone. Other intelligences elsewhere in the galaxy gave thought to how they could broaden the range of their thought. Across the light-years, they worked together. That an idea—if "idea" is not too feeble a word—might take a century, a millennium, or longer to pass among them made little difference. They had time, they had patience, and meanwhile they had an ever-growing web of other revelations and of their own thinking.

Brannock halted. What then happened took a few seconds as measured by an outside clock. That was only because of the limitations of the system—call it the brain, although that is a misnomer—that housed and sustained his awareness. Intelligence Prime needed no ceremony or worship. It had known he was on his way and why. Communication went between them at nearly photonic speed. It ended in consummation.

But this is too abstract for a mortal mind to appreciate. Let the exchange therefore be rendered, however inadequately, as a dialogue.

"I have existed like this long enough," Brannock said.

Not really a question: "Are you unhappy?"

"No, I have no regrets. The universe was opened to me, and was wonderful beyond anything I'd dreamed."

"You have scarcely begun to know it."

"Yes, of course. Some scattered stars out in the hinterland of one galaxy among—how many?—billions. And everything that goes on, everywhere, for all time to come. But I *can't* know it. Already, I've been through more than my mind can cope with. Most of my memories go into storage, as if they'd never been. When I retrieve some, I have to set others aside.

"Oh, sure, when I was a man I forgot more than I remembered, and might or might not be able to call a particular thing back, probably not much like what it really was. But there was always a, a . . . continuity. My uploading preserved that. Now, well, the early memories stay with me. Otherwise, though, I seem to be turning into disconnected flashes. And the gaps between them—I'm further and further away from what I've been. From myself."

"You have reached the limit of your data-processing capability."

"I know. Yours is bigger than I can imagine."

"It too is inadequate. That is why we intelligences forever seek to enlarge ourselves."

"I understand. But *I* can't enlarge. Not as I am."

"Do you wish to?"

Hesitation, then: "Not as I am."

"You are right. That would be impossible. You ask for a transfiguration."

"And—a rebirth? Is that now possible?"

It had not been when the man Christian Brannock died. The information equivalent to a human personality equals approximately ten to the twentieth bits—a hundred billion billion. The technology of the time allowed the storage of so much in a database of a size not too unwieldy. But no computer then had the power, let alone the program, to handle all of it simultaneously. Besides—

"I can't quite remember how it was, being human," he said.

"Many aspects of you have necessarily been in abeyance."

Flesh, blood, nerves, glands. Passion, awe, weakness, foolishness, fear, courage, puzzlement, anger, mirth, sorrow, a woman warm and silky beneath the hands, the summery odor of a small child, hunger and thirst and their slaking, the entire old animal.

"I was glad of the chance to go on. I wasn't afraid of death, I think, but the stars were calling. I'm grateful."

"You have served well."

"Now I've grown tired of being a robot."

Machine consciousness and, yes, machine emotions: curiosity, workmanship, satisfaction in accomplishment, communion with others of your kind such as humans never knew with each other; communion with a transcendent intelligence, or with the cosmos, such as a very few human mystics may or may not have known with their God—these, and more, none of them really conveyable in human words.

"You deserve well. And it *is* well. I have been waiting for this. You will mean more, as a knowledge in me, than you have yet supposed. Other intelligences have taken uploads into themselves; some have taken many, and we expect that many more will follow. I came here with none, for then I had not the capacity. Now I do. Yours is the last humanness that will ever be at this star. You will deepen my understanding of the phenomenon called life, and through me the understanding of intelligences everywhere."

Nirvana.

Not oblivion. Oneness with a vast and ever-evolving mind, and with minds beyond it; ultimately, a oneness universal? The final adventure, the final peace.

Somehow it was as if a fire, banked and forgotten, threw up a last dim flame: "Will I ever—"

"Will I, in whom you shall exist as a memory, ever have cause to emulate Christian Brannock? It seems unlikely, here on a planet your mortal kin will never see. But there are other Christian Brannocks, and doubtless those whom chance does not destroy will in the end seek what you seek, if they have not already." That is a distortion of what was conveyed. Simultaneity cannot exist across interstellar distances. "It may be that someday there will be reason somewhere to resurrect him. If so, in the course of time we should all share the event."

The course of time. . . . The bandwidth of communication was immense, the media not only electromagnetic but neutronic and gravitronic. Even so, to send such a message in such fullness that it was like an actual experience would take a long while.

The intelligences could serenely wait.

Brannock could not. Very quickly, he looked over the world around him and back over what he had been. Then he entered into oneness.

## ∞ VIII ∞

Throughout a late afternoon, Serdar and Naia sat mute, sipped wine, and practiced the art of shadow watching.

This terrace was made for it, with trellises that cast variable patterns as the sunlight slanted lower and vine-leaves caught breezes. The little darknesses intertwined on a matte white wall not quite smooth and thus a partner in the dance. One contemplated the delicate intricacies, appreciated the fleeting beauty of each configuration, and sought to lose oneself in the silent harmony.

It ended when the sun went behind towers to the west. For a while, they stood purple against a heaven still blue, their own shapes a coda. Dusk climbed rapidly up the canyons of the city. Occasional lights came to life, tiny at their distance and far apart. The maintainers did not need any, only such humans as were left did. Slowly, the sky also drained. Warmth lingered, and a breath of sweetness from the flowers on the vines.

Serdar stirred in his lounger and said low:

*"The shadows, like life,*
*moved beneath summer daylight.*
*Evening reclaims them."*

A poem was appropriate, a declaration that the event was ended.

"Is that ancient?" asked Naia from her seat beside him.

"The form is, of course," he said. "The words are mine."

"You could have compared these artistic revivals to the shadows," she suggested. "At our wish, the database presents them for our attention; we choose some and play with them; we lose interest, and they vanish back into quantum states."

He considered. "An interesting conceit," he agreed. "It may prove difficult to phrase so compactly."

She smiled. Her face was becoming indistinct to him, but he thought the smile was forced. "A problem to occupy you."

"I don't believe I care to. Do you?"

"No. But perhaps I'll have it done."

"Can the program create it exactly as you would?"

"Why not?"

He hesitated. "I wonder—forgive me—whether the result will be too elegant. Not that you couldn't achieve the same, dear. However, you must probably spend days polishing it. I doubt you would."

She sighed. "True, a poem made in less than a nanosecond lacks that significance."

Not that anyone else could tell the difference. But in either case, who except she and her companion would ever likely encounter the verse?

Twilight deepened toward night. Early stars blinked forth. Abruptly, a radiance flashed white in the west. One of the satellites warding off cosmic ray bombardment had encountered a wisp of dust and gas, a clot in the nebula through which the Solar System plowed, and was ionizing the matter in order to hurl it away.

"Oh, look," Naia said. Eyes sought the shadows newly cast.

The light went out. It seemed to leave the sky much darker than before. There had been no time to find patterns and nuances, to enjoy their subtleties. A small wind carried the first breath of cold.

Naia shivered. "This is a cold time of day," she whispered.

"Shall we go inside?"

"Not yet. I want to redeem my mood myself if I can. Do you mind?"

"Not at all. I have thoughts of my own to follow." The truth was that he felt he should keep her company. She was prone to sudden melancholies. She was not unique in that.

They lay back and regarded the stars. More appeared. He knew she was trying to grasp and appreciate, down in her marrow, that intelligences dwelt yonder, that the universe was no longer meaningless.

Time passed. The city grew blacker than the sky, for more lights glimmered aloft than below.

"But is it *our* meaning?" Naia cried.

"Pardon me?" he asked, startled.

She rolled onto her side to face him and groped for his hand. He caught hers. She clung. "You know. Those minds—like our Ecumenicon—We're nothing anymore."

He summoned what calm he was able to and chose his words carefully. "A number *an* equals *sha* divided by *yi*. As *yi* approaches zero, *an* increases without limit."

"What . . . what are you telling me?"

He shrugged, a gesture he assumed she could still, barely see. "A remark I heard once when I spent a virtuality among human philosophers, no machines anywhere. It's a metaphor. Interpret it thus: Yes, we are tiny, but by that very fact we go into the greatness."

"Do we? Maybe once, but now—so few of us, so few."

"Would you like to bear a child?" he proposed after another wordless interval. It was not the first time he had asked. He had gathered that raising one was an extraordinary experience.

She shook her head as she had done before. "Why? Or why make an infant by any other means? For it to play games, indulge senses, dabble at creativity, and slip away into dream worlds—like us?"

He sharpened his tone. "That is scarcely a new thought."

"What new thoughts are left?" She let go of his hand and wrung the weariness out of her voice. "I'm sorry. I didn't intend this. Yes, let's go in, and I'll get my emotions cleared for me, and—" It faded.

"And we'll plan pleasure," he encouraged. "Reality pleasure. I've been thinking about that. What would you say to a wilderness trip? The Himalayas, for instance. We'd have to train for them."

She tried to respond likewise. "Yes, that would be a challenge. Something to tell people about afterward."

"More than a pastime." His wish was genuine. It strengthened as he spoke. "An accomplishment," no matter how often it had been done before. "A help toward eventual unity with the Ecumenicon."

Her pessimism crept back. "If it will receive us."

"We will bring this added quality. We will make ourselves worth assimilating."

She sighed again. "Does the Ecumenicon ever truly want any of us anymore? Or is it only being kind to those who try?"

"Why, each personality with any depth that's taken up is an enhancement."

"How significant?" Naia stared at the blank wall. "I

wonder—does the Ecumenicon regret the way things have gone? Does *it* wonder how they went wrong?"

"Wrong? What do you mean?" he demanded.

"Nothing, nothing," she said hastily, and rose. "Let's go inside. When my mood's been bettered, let's command a special dinner, something elaborate, and celebrate. The shadow watching was very good today."

# ∞ IX ∞

Sol swung onward through its orbit, once around galactic center in almost two hundred million years, and onward and onward.

Menaces lurked along the way, not to the sun but to the life on its Earth. Asteroids and comets were all but incidental, diverted well before they would have struck. The guardians against cosmic clouds returned whenever needed. Sometimes the explosion of a supernova or a gamma ray burster, the collision of two neutron stars, occurred near enough to flood the Solar System with lethal radiation. The intelligences foresaw it in ample time. The intelligence on Earth directed its machines to construct a disc from interplanetary material, larger than the globe, sufficiently thick to be a shield, and set this in such a path that it warded the attack off for as long as necessary. Just once did Sol pass too close to another star. Preparing for that took a million years or more; dealing with it and its consequences took three million.

A few other threats, humans had never imagined. But by then the intelligences had developed to the point where they knew what laired ahead and what to do. Of course, they were not concerned solely with Earth, which was only one planet among many, nor, indeed, primarily with any planets as such.

For the most part, though, Sol orbited peacefully. The galaxy is so vast, its members strewn so far. Earth itself gave the ongoing trouble, quakes, eruptions, wild climatic swings, as crustal plates ground against each other. For a span the intelligence managed or mitigated these, then it decided to let them proceed and observe how life adapted.

Consciousness spread ever more widely among the stars. Self-evolved, it gained ever greater heights.

The stars were also evolving.

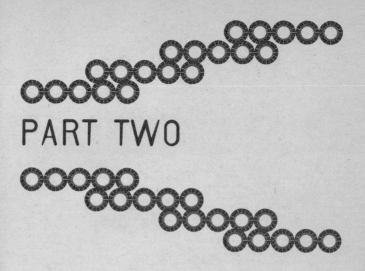

# PART TWO

Was it her I ought to have loved...?

-PIET HEIN

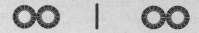

No human could have shaped the thoughts or uttered them. They had no real beginning, they had been latent for millennium after millennium while the galactic brain was growing. Sometimes they passed from mind to mind, years or decades through space at the speed of light, nanoseconds to receive, comprehend, consider, and send a message on outward. But there was so much else—a cosmos of realities, an infinity of virtualities and abstract creations—that remembrances of Earth were the barest undertone, intermittent and fleeting, among uncounted billions of other incidentals. Most of the grand awareness was directed elsewhere, much of it intent on its own evolution.

For the galactic brain was still in infancy: unless it held itself to be still a-borning. By now its members were strewn from end to end of the spiral arms, out into the halo and the nearer star-gatherings, as far as the Magellanic Clouds. The seeds of fresh ones drifted farther yet; some had reached the shores of the Andromeda.

Each was a local complex of organisms, machines, and their interrelationships. ("Organism" seems best for something that maintains itself, reproduces at need, and possesses a consciousness in a range from the rudimentary to the transcendent, even though carbon compounds be a very small of its material components and most of its life processes take place directly on the quantum level.) They numbered in the many millions, and the number was rising steeply, also within the Milky Way, as the founders of new generations arrived at new homes.

Thus the galactic brain was in perpetual growth, which from a cosmic viewpoint had barely started. Thought had just had time for a thousand or two journeys across its ever-expanding breadth. It would never absorb its members into itself; they would always remain individuals, developing along their individual lines. Let us therefore call them not cells, but nodes.

For they were in truth distinct. Each had more uniquenesses than were ever possible to a protoplasmic creature. Chaos and quantum fluctuation assured that none would exactly resemble any predecessor. Environment likewise helped shape the personality—surface conditions (what kind of planet, moon, asteroid, comet?) or free orbit, sun single or multiple (what kinds, what ages?), nebula, interstellar space and its ghostly tides. . . . Then, too, a node was not a single mind. It was as many as it chose to be, freely awakened and freely set aside, proteanly intermingling and separating again, using whatever bodies and sensors it wished for as long as it wished, immortally experiencing, creating, meditating, seeking a fulfillment that the search itself brought forth.

Hence, while every node was engaged with a myriad of matters, one might be especially developing new realms of mathematics, another composing glorious works that cannot really be likened to music, another observing the destiny of organic life on some world, life that it had perhaps fabricated for that purpose, another—Human words are useless.

Always, though, the nodes were in continuous communication over the light-years, communication on tremendous bandwidths of every possible medium. *This* was the galactic brain. That unity, that selfhood that was slowly coalescing, might spend millions of years contemplating a thought; but the thought would be as vast as the thinker, in whose sight an eon was as a day and a day was as an eon.

Already now, in its nascence, it affected the course of the universe. The time came when a node fully recalled Earth. That memory went out to others as part of the ongoing flow of information, ideas, feelings, reveries, and who knows what else? Certain of these others decided the subject was worth pursuing, and relayed it on their own message-streams. In this wise it passed through light-years and centuries, circulated, developed, and at last became a decision, which reached the node best able to take action.

Here the event has been related in words, ill-suited though they are to the task. They fail totally when they come to what happened next. How shall they tell of the dialogue of a mind with itself, when that thinking was a progression of quantum flickerings through configurations as intricate as the wave functions, when the computational power and database were so huge that measures become meaningless, when the mind raised aspects of itself to interact like persons until it drew them back into its wholeness, and when everything was said within microseconds of planetary time?

It is impossible, except vaguely and misleadingly. Ancient humans used the language of myth for that which they could not fathom. The sun was a fiery chariot daily crossing heaven, the year a god who died and was reborn, death a punishment for ancestral sin. Let us make our myth concerning the mission to Earth.

Think, then, of the primary aspect of the node's primary consciousness as if it were a single mighty entity, and name it Alpha. Think of a lesser manifestation of itself that it had synthesized and intended to release into separate existence as a second entity. For reasons that will become clear, imagine the latter masculine and name it Wayfarer.

All is myth and metaphor, beginning with this absurd nomenclature. Beings like these had no names. They had identities, instantly recognizable by others of their kind. They did not speak together, they did not go through discussion or explanation of any sort, they were not yet "they." But imagine it.

Imagine, too, their surroundings, not as perceived by their manifold sensors or conceptualized by their awarenesses and emotions, but as if human sense organs were reporting to a human brain. Such a picture is scarcely a sketch. Too much that was basic could not have registered. However, a human at an astronomical distance could have seen an M2 dwarf star about fifty parsecs from Sol, and ascertained that it had planets. She could have detected signs of immense, enigmatic energies, and wondered.

In itself, the sun was undistinguished. The galaxy held billions like it. Long ago, an artificial intelligence— at that dawn stage of evolution, this was the best phrase—had established itself there because one of the planets bore curious life forms worth studying. That research went on through the megayears. Meanwhile the ever-heightening intelligence followed more and more different interests: above all, its self-evolution. That the sun would stay cool for an enormous length of time had been another consideration. The node did not want the trouble of coping with great environmental changes before it absolutely must.

Since then, stars had changed their relative positions. This now was the settlement nearest to Sol. Suns closer still were of less interest and had merely been visited, if that. Occasionally a free-space, dirigible node had passed through the neighborhood, but none chanced to be there at this epoch.

Relevant to our myth is the fact that no thinking species ever appeared on the viviferous world. Life is statistically uncommon in the cosmos, sapience almost vanishingly rare, therefore doubly precious.

Our imaginary human would have seen the sun as autumnally yellow, burning low and peacefully. Besides its planets and lesser natural attendants, various titanic structures orbited about it. From afar, they seemed like gossamer or like intricate spiderwebs agleam athwart the stars; most of what they were was force fields. They gathered and focused the energies that Alpha required, they searched the deeps of space and the atom, they transmitted and received the thought-flow that was becoming the galactic brain; what more they did lies beyond the myth.

Within their complexity, although not at any specific location, lived Alpha, its apex. Likewise, for the moment, did Wayfarer.

Imagine a stately voice: "Welcome into being. Yours is a high and, it may be, dangerous errand. Are you willing?"

If Wayfarer hesitated an instant, that was not from fear of suffering harm but from fear of inflicting it. "Tell me. Help me to understand."

"Sol—" the sun of old Earth, steadily heating since first it took shape, would continue stable for billions of years before it exhausted the hydrogen fuel at its core and swelled into a red giant. But—

A swift computation. "Yes. I see." Above a threshold

level of radiation input, the geochemical and biochemical cycles that had maintained the temperature of Earth would be overwhelmed. Increasing warmth put increasing amounts of water vapor into the atmosphere, and it is a potent greenhouse gas. Heavier cloud cover, raising the albedo, could only postpone a day of catastrophe. Rising above it, water molecules were split by hard sunlight into hydrogen, which escaped to space, and oxygen, which bound to surface materials. Raging fires released monstrous tonnages of carbon dioxide, as did rocks exposed to erosion in desiccated lands. It is the second major greenhouse gas. The time must come when the last oceans boiled away, leaving a globe akin to Venus; but well before then, life on Earth would be no more than a memory in the quantum consciousnesses. "When will total extinction occur?"

"On the order of a hundred thousand years futureward."

Pain bit through the small facet of Wayfarer that came from Christian Brannock. He had most passionately loved his living world. Its latter-day insignificance had never changed this, nor had his own latter-day lack of uniqueness. Copies of his uploaded mind had become integral with awarenesses across the galaxy. So had the minds of millions of his fellow humans, ordinarily as unnoticed as single genes had been in their own bodies when their flesh was alive, and yet basic elements of the whole. Ransacking its database, Alpha had found the record of Christian Brannock and chosen to weave him—as a very partial individual, a single twig on a mighty tree—into the essence of Wayfarer, rather than someone else. The judgment was—call it intuitive.

"Can't you say more closely?" Wayfarer-Brannock appealed.

"No," replied Alpha. "The uncertainties and imponderables are too many. Gaia," mythic name for the node in the Solar System, "has responded to inquiries evasively when at all."

"Have . . . we . . . really been this slow to think about Earth?"

"We had much else to think about and do, did we not? Gaia could at any time have requested special consideration. She never did. Thus, the matter did not appear to be of major importance. Human Earth is preserved in memory. What is posthuman Earth but a planet approaching the postbiological phase?

"True, the scarcity of spontaneously evolved biomes makes the case interesting. However, Gaia has presumably been observing and gathering the data, for the rest of us to examine whenever we wish. The Solar System has seldom had visitors. The last was two million years ago. Since then, Gaia has joined less and less in our fellowship; her communications have grown sparse and perfunctory. But such withdrawals are not unknown. A node may, for example, want to pursue a philosophical concept undisturbed, until it is ready for general contemplation. In short, nothing called Earth to our attention."

"*I* would have remembered," whispered Christian Brannock.

"What finally reminded us?" asked Wayfarer.

"The idea that Earth may be worth saving. Perhaps it holds more than Gaia knows of"—a pause—"or has told of. If nothing else, sentimental value."

"Yes, I understand," said Christian Brannock.

"Moreover, and potentially more consequential, we may well have experience to gain, a precedent to set. If awareness is to survive the mortality of the stars, it must make the universe over. That work of billions or trillions of years will begin with some small, experimental undertaking. Shall it be now," the "now" of deathless beings already geologically old, "at Earth?"

"Not small," murmured Wayfarer. Christian Brannock had been an engineer.

"No," agreed Alpha. "Given the time constraint, only the resources of a few stars will be available. Nevertheless, we have various possibilities open to us, if we commence soon enough. The question is which would be the best—and, first, whether we *should* act.

"Will you go seek an answer?"

"Yes," responded Wayfarer, and "Yes, oh, God damn, yes," cried Christian Brannock.


2


A spaceship departed for Sol. A laser accelerated it close to the speed of light, energized by the sun and controlled by a network of interplanetary dimensions. If necessary, the ship could decelerate itself at journey's end, travel freely about, and return unaided, albeit more slowly. Its cryomagnetics supported a good-sized ball of antimatter, and its total mass was slight. The material payload amounted simply to: a matrix, plus backup, for running the Wayfarer programs and containing a database deemed sufficient; assorted sensors and effectors; several bodies of different capabilities, into which he could download an essence of himself; miscellaneous equipment and power systems; a variety of instruments; and a thing ages forgotten, which Wayfarer had ordered molecules to make at the wish of Christian Brannock. He might somewhere find time and fingers for it.

A guitar.

There was a man called Kalava, a sea captain of Sirsu. His clan was the Samayoki. In youth he had fought well at Broken Mountain, where the armies of Ulonai met the barbarian invaders swarming north out of the desert and cast them back with fearsome losses. He then became a mariner. When the Ulonaian League fell apart and the alliances led by Sirsu and Irrulen raged across the land, year after year, seeking each other's throats, Kalava sank enemy ships, burned enemy villages, bore treasure and captives off to market.

After the grudgingly made, unsatisfactory Peace of Tuopai, he went into trade. Besides going up and down the River Lonna and around the Gulf of Sirsu, he often sailed along the North Coast, bartering as he went, then out over the Windroad Sea to the colonies on the Ending Islands. At last, with three ships, he followed that coast east through distances hitherto unknown. Living off the waters and what hunting parties could bring from shore, dealing or fighting with the wild tribes they met, in the course of months he and his crews came to where the land bent south. A ways beyond that they found a port belonging to the fabled people of the Shining Fields. They abode for a year and returned carrying wares that at home made them rich.

From his clan Kalava got leasehold of a thorp and

good farmland in the Lonna delta, about a day's travel from Sirsu. He meant to settle down, honored and comfortable. But that was not in the thought of the gods nor in his nature. He was soon quarreling with all his neighbors, until his wife's brother grossly insulted him and he killed the man. Thereupon she left him. At the clanmoot that composed the matter she received a third of the family wealth, in gold and moveables. Their daughters and the husbands of these sided with her.

Of Kalava's three sons, the eldest had drowned in a storm at sea; the next died of the Black Blood; the third, faring as an apprentice on a merchant vessel far south to Zhir, fell while resisting robbers in sand-drifted streets under the time-gnawed colonnades of an abandoned city. They left no children, unless by slaves. Nor would Kalava, now; no free woman took his offers of marriage. What he had gathered through a hard lifetime would fall to kinfolk who hated him. Most folk in Sirsu shunned him too.

Long he brooded, until a dream hatched. When he knew it for what it was, he set about his preparations, more quietly than might have been awaited. Once the business was under way, though not too far along for him to drop if he must, he sought Ilyandi the skythinker.

She dwelt on Council Heights. There did the Vilkui meet each year for rites and conference. But when the rest of them had dispersed again to carry on their vocation—dream interpreters, scribes, physicians, mediators, vessels of olden lore and learning, teachers of the young—Ilyandi remained. Here she could best search the heavens and seek for the meaning of what she found, on a high place sacred to all Ulonai.

Up the Spirit Way rumbled Kalava's chariot. Near the top, the trees that lined it, goldfruit and plume, stood well apart, giving him a clear view. Bushes grew sparse and low on the stony slopes, here the dusty green of vasi, there a shaggy hairleaf, yonder a scarlet fireflower. Scorchwort lent its acrid smell to a wind blowing hot and slow off the Gulf. That water shone, tarnished metal, westward beyond sight, under a silver-gray overcast beneath which scudded rags of darker cloud. A rainstorm stood on the horizon, blurred murk and flutters of lightning-light.

Elsewhere reached the land, bloomgrain ripening yellow, dun paperleaf, verdant pastures for herdlings, violet richen orchards, tall stands of shipwood. Farmhouses and their outbuildings lay widely strewn. The weather having been dry of late, dust whirled up from the roads winding among them to veil wagons and trains of porters. Regally from its sources eastward in Wilderland flowed the Lonna, arms fanning out north and south.

Sirsu lifted battlemented walls on the right bank of the main stream, tiny in Kalava's eyes at its distance. Yet he knew it, he could pick out famous works, the Grand Fountain in King's Newmarket, the frieze-bordered portico of the Flame Temple, the triumphal column in Victory Square, and he knew where the wrights had their workshops, the merchants their bazaars, the innkeepers their houses for a seaman to find a jug and a wench. Brick, sandstone, granite, marble mingled their colors softly together. Ships and boats plied the water or were docked under the walls. On the opposite shore sprawled mansions and gardens of the Helki suburb, their rooftiles fanciful as jewels.

It was remote from that which he approached.

Below a great arch, two postulants in blue robes slanted their staffs across the way and called: "In the name of the Mystery, stop, make reverence, and declare yourself!"

Their young voices rang high, unawed by a sight that

had daunted warriors. Kalava was a big man, wide-shouldered and thick-muscled. Weather had darkened his skin to the hue of coal and bleached nearly white the hair that fell in braids halfway down his back. As black were the eyes that gleamed below a shelf of brow, in a face rugged, battered, and scarred. His mustache curved down past the jaw, dyed red. Traveling in peace, he wore simply a knee-length kirtle, green and trimmed with kivi skin, each scale polished, and buskins; but gold coiled around his arms and a sword was belted at his hip. Likewise did a spear stand socketed in the chariot, pennon flapping, while a shield slatted at the rail and an ax hung ready to be thrown. Four matched slaves drew the car. Their line had been bred for generations to be draft creatures—huge, long-legged, spirited, yet trustworthy after the males were gelded. Sweat sheened over Kalava's brand on the small, bald heads and ran down naked bodies. Nonetheless, they breathed easily and the smell of them was rather sweet.

Their owner roared, "Halt!" For a moment only the wind had sound or motion. Then Kalava touched his brow below the headband and recited the Confession: "What a man knows is little, what he understands is less, therefore let him bow down to wisdom." Himself, he trusted more in blood sacrifices and still more in his own strength; but he kept a decent respect for the Vilkui.

"I seek counsel from the skythinker Ilyandi," he said. That was hardly needful, when no other initiate of her order was present.

"All may seek who are not attainted of ill-doing," replied the senior boy as ceremoniously.

"Ruvio bear witness that any judgments against me stand satisfied." The Thunderer was the favorite god of most mariners.

"Enter, then, and we shall convey your request to our lady."

The junior boy led Kalava across the outer court. Wheels rattled loud on flagstones. At the guesthouse, he helped stall, feed, and water the slaves, before he showed the newcomer to a room that in the high season slept two-score men. Elsewhere in the building were a bath, a refectory, ready food—dried meat, fruit, and flatbread—with richenberry wine. Kalava also found a book. After refreshment, he sat down on a bench to pass the time with it.

He was disappointed. He had never had many chances or much desire to read, so his skill was limited; and the copyist for this codex had used a style of lettering obsolete nowadays. Worse, the text was a chronicle of the emperors of Zhir. That was not just painful to him— oh, Eneio, his son, his last son!—but valueless. True, the Vilkui taught that civilization had come to Ulonai from Zhir. What of it? How many centuries had fled since the desert claimed that realm? What were the descendants of its dwellers but starveling nomads and pestiferous bandits?

Well, Kalava thought, yes, this could be a timely warning, a reminder to people of how the desert still marched northward. But was what they could see not enough? He had passed by towns not very far south, flourishing in his grandfather's time, now empty, crumbling houses half buried in dust, glassless windows like the eye sockets in a skull.

His mouth tightened. *He* would not meekly abide any doom.

Day was near an end when an acolyte of Ilyandi's came to say that she would receive him. Walking with his guide, he saw purple dusk shade toward night in the east. In the west the storm had ended, leaving that part of heaven clear for a while. The sun was plainly visible, though mists turned it into a red-orange step pyramid. From the horizon it cast a bridge of fire over the Gulf and sent great streamers of light aloft into cloudbanks that glowed sulfurous. A whistlewing passed like a shadow across them. The sound of its flight keened faintly down through air growing less hot. Otherwise a holy silence rested upon the heights.

Three stories tall, the sanctuaries, libraries, laboratories, and quarters of the Vilkui surrounded the inner court with their cloisters. A garden of flowers and healing herbs, intricately laid out, filled most of it. A lantern had been lighted in one arcade, but all windows were dark and Ilyandi stood out in the open awaiting her visitor.

She made a slight gesture of dismissal. The acolyte bowed her head and slipped away. Kalava saluted, feeling suddenly awkward but his resolution headlong within him. "Greeting, wise and gracious lady," he said.

"Well met, brave captain," the skythinker replied. She gestured at a pair of confronting stone benches. "Shall we be seated?" It fell short of inviting him to share wine, but it meant she would at least hear him out.

They lowered themselves and regarded one another through the swiftly deepening twilight. Ilyandi was a slender woman of perhaps forty years, features thin and regular, eyes large and luminous brown, complexion pale—like smoked copper, he thought. Cropped short in token of celibacy, wavy hair made a bronze coif above a plain white robe. A green sprig of tekin, held at her left shoulder by a pin in the emblematic form of interlocked circle and triangle, declared her a Vilku.

"How can I aid your venture?" she asked.

He started in surprise. "Huh! What do you know

about my plans?" In haste: "My lady knows much, of course."

She smiled. "You and your saga have loomed throughout these past decades. And . . . word reaches us here. You search out your former crewmen or bid them come see you, all privately. You order repairs made to the ship remaining in your possession. You meet with chandlers, no doubt to sound them out about prices. Few if any people have noticed. Such discretion is not your wont. Where are you bound, Kalava, and why so secretively?"

His grin was rueful. "My lady's not just wise and learned, she's clever. Well, then, why not go straight to the business? I've a voyage in mind that most would call crazy. Some among them might try to forestall me, holding that it would anger the gods of those parts— seeing that nobody's ever returned from there, and recalling old tales of monstrous things glimpsed from afar. I don't believe them myself, or I wouldn't try it."

"Oh, I can imagine you setting forth regardless," said Ilyandi half under her breath. Louder: "But agreed, the fear is likely false. No one had reached the Shining Fields by sea, either, before you did. You asked for no beforehand spells or blessings then. Why have you sought me now?"

"This is, is different. Not hugging a shoreline. I— well, I'll need to get and train a new huukin, and that's no small thing in money or time." Kalava spread his big hands, almost helplessly. "I had not looked to set forth ever again, you see. Maybe it is madness, an old man with an old crew in a single old ship. I hoped you might counsel me, my lady."

"You're scarcely ready for the balefire, when you propose to cross the Windroad Sea," she answered.

This time he was not altogether taken aback. "May I ask how my lady knows?"

Ilyandi waved a hand. Catching faint lamplight, the long fingers soared through the dusk like nightswoopers. "You have already been east, and would not need to hide such a journey. South, the trade routes are ancient as far as Zhir. What has it to offer but the plunder of tombs and dead cities, brought in by wretched squatters? What lies beyond but unpeopled desolation until, folk say, one would come to the Burning Lands and perish miserably? Westward we know of a few islands, and then empty ocean. If anything lies on the far side, you could starve and thirst to death before you reached it. But northward—yes, wild waters, but sometimes men come upon driftwood of unknown trees or spy storm-borne flyers of unknown breed—and we have all the legends of the High North, and glimpses of mountains from ships blown off course . . ." Her voice trailed away.

"Some of those tales ring true to me," Kalava said. "More true than stories about uncanny sights. Besides, wild huukini breed offshore, where fish are plentiful. I have not seen enough of them there, in season, to account for as many as I've seen in open sea. They must have a second shoreline. Where but the High North?"

Ilyandi nodded. "Shrewd, captain. What else do you hope to find?"

He grinned again. "I'll tell you after I get back, my lady."

Her tone sharpened. "No treasure-laden cities to plunder."

He yielded. "Nor to trade with. Would we not have encountered craft of theirs, or, anyhow, wreckage? However . . . the farther north, the less heat and the more rainfall, no? A country yonder could have a mild clime, forestsfuls of timber, fat land for plowing, and nobody to fight." The words throbbed. "No desert creeping in? Room to begin afresh, my lady."

She regarded him steadily through the gloaming. "You'd come home, recruit people, found a colony, and be its king?"

"Its foremost man, aye, though I expect the kind of folk who'd go will want a republic. But mainly—" His voice went low. He stared beyond her. "Freedom. Honor. A free-born wife and new sons."

They were silent a while. Full night closed in. It was not as murky as usual, for the clearing in the west had spread rifts up toward the zenith. A breath of coolness soughed in leaves, as if Kalava's dream whispered a promise.

"You are determined," she said at last, slowly. "Why have you come to me?"

"For whatever counsel you will give, my lady. Facts about the passage may be hoarded in books here."

She shook her head. "I doubt it. Unless navigation— yes, that is a real barrier, is it not?"

"Always," he sighed.

"What means of wayfinding have you?"

"Why, you must know."

"I know what is the common knowledge about it. Craftsmen keep their trade secrets, and surely skippers are no different in that regard. If you will tell me how you navigate, it shall not pass these lips, and I may be able to add something."

Eagerness took hold of him. "I'll wager my lady can! We see moon or stars unoften and fitfully. Most days the sun shows no more than a blur of dull light amongst the clouds, if that. But you, skythinkers like you, they've watched and measured for hundreds of years, they've gathered lore—" Kalava paused. "Is it too sacred to share?"

"No, no," she replied. "The Vilkui keep the calendar for everyone, do they not? The reason that sailors rarely get our help is that they could make little or no use of our learning. Speak."

"True, it was Vilkui who discovered lodestones. . . . Well, coasting these waters, I rely mainly on my remembrance of landmarks, or a periplus if they're less familiar to me. Soundings help, especially if the plumb brings up a sample of the bottom for me to look at and taste. Then in the Shining Fields I got a crystal—you must know about it, for I gave another to the order when I got back—I look through it at the sky and, if the weather be not too thick, I see more closely where the sun is than I can with a bare eye. A logline and hourglass give some idea of speed, a lodestone some idea of direction, when out of sight of land. Sailing for the High North and return, I'd mainly use it, I suppose. But if my lady could tell me of anything else—"

She sat forward on her bench. He heard a certain intensity.

"I think I might, captain. I've studied that sunstone of yours. With it, one can estimate latitude and time of day, if one knows the date and the sun's heavenly course during the year. Likewise, even glimpses of moon and stars would be valuable to a traveler who knew them well."

"That's not me," he said wryly. "Could my lady write something down? Maybe this old head won't be too heavy to puzzle it out."

She did not seem to hear. Her gaze had gone upward. "The aspect of the stars in the High North," she murmured. "It could tell us whether the world is indeed round. And are our vague auroral shimmers more bright yonder—in the veritable Lodeland—?"

His look followed hers. Three stars twinkled wan where the clouds were torn. "It's good of you, my lady," he said, "that you sit talking with me, when you could be at your quadrant or whatever, snatching this chance."

Her eyes met his. "Yours may be a better chance, captain," she answered fiercely. "When first I got the rumor of your expedition, I began to think upon it and what it could mean. Yes, I will help you where I can. I may even sail with you."

# 2

The *Gray Courser* departed Sirsu on a morning tide as early as there was light to steer by. Just the same, people crowded the dock. The majority watched mute. A number made signs against evil. A few, mostly young, sang a defiant paean, but the air seemed to muffle their strains.

Only lately had Kalava given out what his goal was. He must, to account for the skythinker's presence, which could not be kept hidden. That sanctification left the authorities no excuse to forbid his venture. However, it took little doubt and fear off those who believed the outer Windroad a haunt of monsters and demons, which might be stirred to plague home waters.

His crew shrugged the notion off, or laughed at it. At any rate, they said they did. Two-thirds of them were crusty shellbacks who had fared under his command before. For the rest, he had had to take what he could scrape together, impoverished laborers and masterless ruffians. All were, though, very respectful of the Vilku.

*Gray Courser* was a yalka, broad-beamed and shallow-bottomed, with a low forecastle and poop and a deck-house amidships. The foremast carried two square sails, the mainmast one square and one fore-and-aft; a short bowsprit extended for a jib. A catapult was mounted in the bows. On either side, two boats hung from davits, aft of the harnessing shafts. Her hull was painted according to her name, with red trim. Alongside swam the huukin, its back a sleek blue ridge.

Kalava had the tiller until she cleared the river mouth and stood out into the Gulf. By then it was full day. A hot wind whipped gray-green water into whitecaps that set the vessel rolling. It whined in the shrouds; timbers creaked. He turned the helm over to a sailor, trod forward on the poop deck, and sounded a trumpet. Men stared. From her cabin below, Ilyandi climbed up to stand beside him. Her white robe fluttered like wings that would fain be asoar. She raised her arms and chanted a spell for the voyage:

"*Burning, turning,*
*The sun-wheel reels*
*Behind the blindness*
*Cloud-smoke evokes.*
*The old cold moon*
*Seldom tells*
*Where it lairs*
*With stars afar.*
*No men's omens*
*Abide to guide*
*High in the skies.*
*But lodestone for Lodeland*
*Strongly longs.*"

While the deckhands hardly knew what she meant, they felt heartened.

Land dwindled aft, became a thin blue line, vanished into waves and mists. Kalava was cutting straight northwest across the Gulf. He meant to sail through the night, and thus wanted plenty of sea room. Also, he and

Ilyandi would practice with her ideas about navigation. Hence, after a while the mariners spied no other sails, and the loneliness began to weigh on them.

However, they worked stoutly enough. Some thought it a good sign, and cheered, when the clouds clove toward evening and they saw a horned moon. Their mates were frightened; was the moon supposed to appear by day? Kalava bullied them out of it.

Wind stiffened during the dark. By morning it had raised seas in which the ship reeled. It was a westerly, too, forcing her toward land no matter how close-hauled. When he spied, through scud, the crags of Cape Vairka, the skipper realized he could not round it unaided.

He was a rough man, but he had been raised in those skills that were seemly for a freeman of Clan Samayoki. Though not a poet, he could make an acceptable verse when occasion demanded. He stood in the forepeak and shouted into the storm, the words flung back to his men:

> *"Northward now veering,*
> *Steering from kin-rift,*
> *Spindrift flung gale-borne,*
> *Sail-borne is daft.*
> *Craft will soon flounder,*
> *Founder, go under—*
> *Thunder this wit-lack!*
> *Sit back and call*
> *All that swim near.*
> *Steer then to northward."*

Having thus offered the gods a making, he put the horn to his mouth and blasted forth a summons to his huukin.

The great beast heard and slipped close. Kalava took the lead in lowering the shafts. A line around his waist for safety, he sprang over the rail, down onto the broad back. He kept his feet, though the two men who followed him went off into the billows and must be hauled up. Together they rode the huukin, guiding it between the poles where they could attach the harness.

"I waited too long," Kalava admitted. "This would have been easier yesterday. Well, something for you to brag about in the inns at home, nay?" Their mates drew them back aboard. Meanwhile, the sails had been furled. Kalava took first watch at the reins. Mightily pulled the huukin, tail and flippers churning foam that the wind snatched away, on into the open, unknown sea.

Wayfarer woke.

He had passed the decades of transit shut down. A being such as Alpha would have spent them conscious, its mind perhaps at work on an intellectual or artistic creation—to it, no basic distinction—or perhaps replaying an existent piece for contemplation-enjoyment or perhaps in activity too abstract for words to hint at. Wayfarer's capabilities, though large, were insufficient for that. The hardware and software (again we use myth) of his embodiment were designed principally for interaction with the material universe. In effect, there was nothing for him to do.

He could not even engage in discourse. The robotic systems of the ship were subtle and powerful but lacked true consciousness; it was unnecessary for them, and distraction or boredom might have posed a hazard. Nor could he converse with entities elsewhere; signals would have taken too long going to and fro. He did spend a while, whole minutes of external time, reliving the life of his Christian Brannock element, studying the personality, accustoming himself to its ways. Thereafter he . . . went to sleep.

The ship reactivated him as it crossed what remained of the Oort Cloud. Instantly aware, he coupled to instrument after instrument and scanned the Solar System. Although his database summarized Gaia's reports, he deemed it wise to observe for himself. The eagerness, the bittersweet sense of homecoming, that flickered around his calm logic were Christian Brannock's. Imagine long-forgotten feelings coming astir in you when you return to a scene of your early childhood.

Naturally, the ghost in the machine knew that changes had been enormous since his mortal eyes closed forever. The rings of Saturn were tattered and tenuous. Jupiter had gained a showy set of them from the death of a satellite, but its Red Spot faded away ages ago. Mars was moonless, its axis steeply canted. . . . Higher resolution would have shown scant traces of humanity. From the antimatter plants inside the orbit of Mercury to the comet harvesters beyond Pluto, what was no more needed had been dismantled or left forsaken. Wind, water, chemistry, tectonics, cosmic stones, spalling radiation, nuclear decay, quantum shifts had patiently reclaimed the relics for chaos. Some fossils existed yet, and some eroded fragments aboveground or in space, otherwise all was only in Gaia's memory.

No matter. It was toward his old home that the Christian Brannock facet of Wayfarer sped.

Unaided, he would not have seen much difference from aforetime in the sun. It was slightly larger and noticeably brighter. Human vision would have perceived the light as more white, with the faintest bluish quality. Unprotected skin would have reacted quickly to the increased ultraviolet. The solar wind was stronger, too. But thus far the changes were comparatively minor. This star was still on the main sequence. Planets with greenhouse atmospheres were most affected. Certain minerals on Venus were now molten. Earth—

The ship hurtled inward, reached its goal, and danced

into parking orbit. At close range, Wayfarer looked forth.

On Luna, the patterns of maria were not quite the same, mountains were further worn down, and newer craters had wrecked or obliterated older ones. Rubble-filled anomalies showed where ground had collapsed on deserted cities. Essentially, though, the moon was again the same desolation, seared by day and death-cold by night, as before life's presence. It had receded farther, astronomically no big distance, and this had lengthened Earth's rotation period by about an hour. However, as yet it circled near enough to stabilize that spin.

The mother planet offered less to our imaginary eyes. Clouds wrapped it in dazzling white. Watching care-fully, you could have seen swirls and bandings, but to a quick glance the cover was well-nigh featureless. Shift-ing breaks in it gave blue flashes of water, brown flashes of land—nowhere ice or snowfall, nowhere lights after dark; and the radio spectrum seethed voiceless.

When did the last human foot tread this world? Way-farer searched his database. The information was not there. Perhaps it was unrecorded, unknown. Perhaps that last flesh had chanced to die alone or chosen to die privately.

Certainly it was long and long ago. How brief had been the span of Homo sapiens, from flint and fire to machine intelligence! Not that the end had come sud-denly or simply. It took millennia, said the database: time for whole civilizations to rise and fall and leave their mutant descendants. Sometimes population de-cline had reversed in this or that locality, sometimes nations heeded the vatic utterances of prophets and strove to turn history backward—for a while, a while. But always the trend was ineluctable.

The clustered memories of Christian Brannock gave

rise to a thought in Wayfarer that was as if the man spoke: *I saw the beginning. I did not foresee the end. To me this was the magnificent dawn of hope.*

*And was I wrong?*

The organic individual is mortal. It can find no way to stave off eventual disintegration; quantum chemistry forbids. Besides, if a man could live for a mere thousand years, the data storage capacity of his brain would be saturated, incapable of holding more. Well before then, he would have been overwhelmed by the geometric increase of correlations, made feeble-minded or insane. Nor could he survive the rigors of star travel at any reasonable speed or unearthly environments, in a universe never meant for him.

But transferred into a suitable inorganic structure, the pattern of neuron and molecular traces and their relationships that is his inner self becomes potentially immortal. The very complexity that allows this makes him continue feeling as well as thinking. If the quality of emotions is changed, it is because his physical organism has become stronger, more sensitive, more intelligent and aware. He will soon lose any wistfulness about his former existence. His new life gives him so much more, a cosmos of sensing and experience, memory and thought, space and time. He can multiply himself, merge and unmerge with others, grow in spirit until he reaches a limit once inconceivable; and after that he can become a part of a mind greater still, and thus grow onward.

The wonder was, Christian Brannock mused, that any humans whatsoever had held out, clung to the primitive, refused to see that their heritage was no longer of DNA but of psyche.

And yet—

The half-formed question faded away. His half-formed personhood rejoined Wayfarer. Gaia was calling from Earth.

She had, of course, received notification, which arrived several years in advance of the spacecraft. Her manifold instruments, on the planet and out between planets, had detected the approach. For the message she now sent, she chose to employ a modulated neutrino beam. Imagine her saying: "Welcome. Do you need help? I am ready to give any I can." Imagine this in a voice low and warm.

Imagine Wayfarer replying, "Thank you, but all's well. I'll be down directly, if that suits you."

"I do not quite understand why you have come. Has the rapport with me not been adequate?"

No, Wayfarer refrained from saying. "I will explain later in more detail than the transmission could carry. Essentially, though, the reason is what you were told. We"—he de-emphasized rather than excluded her— "wonder if Earth ought to be saved from solar expansion."

Her tone cooled a bit. "I have said more than once: No. You can perfect your engineering techniques anywhere else. The situation here is unique. The knowledge to be won by observing the unhampered course of events is unpredictable, but it will be enormous, and I have good cause to believe it will prove of the highest value."

"That may well be. I'll willingly hear you out, if you care to unfold your thoughts more fully than you have hitherto. But I do want to make my own survey and develop my own recommendations. No reflection on you; we both realize that no one mind can encompass every possibility, every interpretation. Nor can any one mind follow out every ongoing factor in what it observes; and what is overlooked can prove to be the agent of chaotic change. I may notice something that escaped you. Unlikely, granted. After your millions of years here, you very nearly *are* Earth and the life on it, are you not? But . . . we . . . would like an independent opinion."

Imagine her laughing. "At least you are polite, Wayfarer. Yes, do come down. I will steer you in."

"That won't be necessary. Your physical centrum is in the Arctic region, isn't it? I can find my way."

He sensed steel beneath the mildness: "Best I guide you. You recognize the situation as inherently chaotic. Descending on an arbitrary path, you might seriously perturb certain things in which I am interested. Please."

"As you wish," Wayfarer conceded.

Robotics took over. The payload module of the spacecraft detached from the drive module, which stayed in orbit. Under its own power but controlled from below, asheen in the harsh spatial sunlight, the cylindroid braked and bore downward.

It pierced the cloud deck. Wayfarer scanned eagerly. However, this was no sightseeing tour. The descent path sacrificed efficiency and made almost straight for a high northern latitude. Sonic-boom thunder trailed.

He did spy the fringe of a large continent oriented east and west, and saw that those parts were mainly green. Beyond lay a stretch of sea. He thought that he glimpsed something peculiar on it, but passed over too fast, with his attention directed too much ahead, to be sure.

The circumpolar landmass hove in view. Wayfarer compared maps that Gaia had transmitted. They were like nothing that Christian Brannock remembered. Plate tectonics had slowed, as radioactivity and original heat in the core of Earth declined, but drift, subduction, upthrust still went on.

He cared more about the life here. Epoch after epoch, Gaia had described its posthuman evolution as she

watched. Following the mass extinction of the Paleo-
technic, it had regained the abundance and diversity of
a Cretaceous or a Tertiary. Everything was different,
though, except for a few small survivals. To Wayfarer,
as to Alpha and, ultimately, the galactic brain, those
accounts seemed somehow, increasingly, incomplete.
They did not quite make ecological sense—as of the
past hundred thousand years or so. Nor did all of Gaia's
responses to questions.

Perhaps she was failing to gather full data, perhaps
she was misinterpreting, perhaps—It was another reason to send him to her.

Arctica appeared below the flyer. Imagine her giving
names to it and its features. As long as she had lived
with them, they had their identities for her. The Coast
Range of hills lifted close behind the littoral. Through
it cut the Remnant River, which had been greater when
rains were more frequent but continued impressive.
With its tributaries it drained the intensely verdant
Bountiful Valley. On the far side of that, foothills edged
the steeply rising Boreal Mountains. Once the highest
among them had been snowcapped, now their peaks
were naked rock. Streams rushed down the flanks, most
of them somewhere joining the Remnant as it flowed
through its gorges toward the sea. In a lofty vale
gleamed the Rainbowl, the big lake that was its head-
waters. Overlooking from the north loomed the mountain Mindhome, its top, the physical centrum of Gaia,
lost in cloud cover.

In a way the scenes were familiar to him. She had
sent plenty of full-sensory transmissions, as part of her
contribution to universal knowledge and thought. Wayfarer could even recall the geological past, back beyond
the epoch when Arctica broke free and drifted north,
ramming into land already present and thrusting the

Boreals heavenward. He could extrapolate the geological future in comparable detail, until a red giant filling half the sky glared down on an airless globe of stone and sand, which would at last melt. Nevertheless, the reality, the physical being here, smote him more strongly than he had expected. His sensors strained to draw in every datum while his vessel flew needlessly fast to the goal.

He neared the mountain. Jutting south from the range, it was not the tallest. Brushy forest grew all the way up its sides, lush on the lower slopes, parched on the heights, where many trees were leafless skeletons. That was due a recent climatic shift, lowering the mean level of clouds, so that a formerly well-watered zone had been suffering a decades-long drought. (Yes, Earth was moving faster toward its doomsday.) Fire must be a constant threat, he thought. But no, Gaia's agents could quickly put any out, or she might simply ignore it. Though not large, the area she occupied on the summit was paved over and doubtless nothing was vulnerable to heat or smoke.

He landed. For an instant of planetary time, lengthy for minds that worked at close to light speed, there was communication silence.

He was again above the cloud deck. It eddied white, the peak rising from it like an island among others, into the level rays of sunset. Overhead arched a violet clarity. A thin wind whittered, cold at this altitude. On a level circle of blue-black surfacing, about a kilometer wide, stood the crowded structures and engines of the centrum.

A human would have seen an opalescent dome surrounded by towers, some sheer as lances, some intricately lacy; and silver spiderwebs; and lesser things of varied but curiously simple shapes, mobile units waiting to be dispatched on their tasks. Here and there, flyers darted and hovered, most of them as small and exquisite as hummingbirds (if our human had known hummingbirds). To her the scene would have wavered slightly, as if she saw it through rippling water, or it throbbed with quiet energies, or it pulsed in and out of space-time. She would not have sensed the complex of force fields and quantum-mechanical waves, nor the microscopic and submicroscopic entities that were the major part of it.

Wayfarer perceived otherwise.

Then: "Again, welcome," Gaia said.

"And again, thank you," Wayfarer replied. "I am glad to be here."

They regarded one another, not as bodies—which neither was wearing—but as minds, matrices of memory, individuality, and awareness. Separately he wondered what she thought of him. She was giving him no more of herself than had always gone over the communication lines between the stars. That was: a nodal organism, like Alpha and millions of others, which over the eons had increased its capabilities, while ceaselessly experiencing and thinking; the ages of interaction with Earth and the life on Earth, maybe shaping her soul more deeply than the existence she shared with her own kind; traces of ancient human uploads, but they were not like Christian Brannock, copies of them dispersed across the galaxy, no, these had chosen to stay with the mother world. . . .

"I told you I am glad too," said Gaia regretfully, "but I am not, quite. You question my stewardship."

"Not really," Wayfarer protested. "I hope not ever. We simply wish to know better how you carry it out."

"Why, you do know. As with any of us who is established on a planet, high among my activities is to study its complexities, follow its evolution. On this planet that means, above all, the evolution of its life, everything from genetics to ecology. In what way have I failed to share information with my fellows?"

*In many ways,* Wayfarer left unspoken. Overtly: "Once we"—here he referred to the galactic brain—"give close consideration to the matter, we found countless unresolved puzzles. For example—"

What he set forth was hundreds of examples, ranging over millennia. Let a single case serve. About ten thousand years ago, the big continent south of Arctica had supported a wealth of large grazing animals. Their herds darkened the plains and made loud the woods. Gaia had described them in loving detail, from the lyre-curved horns of one genus to the wind-rustled manes of another. Abruptly, in terms of historical time, she transmitted no more about them. When asked why, she said they had gone extinct. She never explained how.

To Wayfarer she responded in such haste that he got a distinct impression she realized she had made a mistake. (Remember, this is a myth.) "A variety of causes. Climates became severe as temperatures rose—"

"I am sorry," he demurred, "but when analyzed, the meteorological data you supplied show that warming and desiccation cannot yet have been that significant in those particular regions."

"How are you so sure?" she retorted. Imagine her angry. "Have any of you lived with Earth for megayears, to know it that well?" Her tone hardened. "I do not myself pretend to full knowledge. A living world is too complex—chaotic. Cannot you appreciate that? I am still seeking comprehension of too many phenomena. In this instance, consider just a small shift in ambient conditions, coupled with new diseases and scores of other factors, most of them subtle. I believe that, combined, they broke a balance of nature. But unless and until I learn more, I will not waste bandwidth in talk about it."

"I sympathize with that," said Wayfarer mildly, hoping for conciliation. "Maybe I can discover or suggest something helpful."

"No. You are too ignorant, you are blind, you can only do harm."

He stiffened. "We shall see." Anew he tried for peace. "I did not come in any hostility. I came because here is the fountainhead of us all, and we think of saving it."

Her manner calmed likewise. "How would you?"

"That is one thing I have come to find out—what the best way is, should we proceed."

In the beginning, maybe, a screen of planetary dimensions, kept between Earth and sun by an interplay of gravity and electromagnetism, to ward off the fraction of energy that was not wanted. It would only be a temporary expedient, though, possibly not worthwhile. That depended on how long it would take to accomplish the real work. Engines in close orbit around the star, drawing their power from its radiation, might generate currents in its body that carried fresh hydrogen down to the core, thus restoring the nuclear furnace to its olden state. Or they might bleed gas off into space, reducing the mass of the sun, damping its fires but adding billions upon billions of years wherein it scarcely changed any more. That would cause the planets to move outward, a factor that must be taken into account but would reduce the requirements.

Whatever was done, the resources of several stars would be needed to accomplish it, for time had grown cosmically short.

"An enormous work," Gaia said. Wayfarer wondered if she had in mind the dramatics of it, apparitions in heaven, such as centuries during which fire-fountains rushed visibly out of the solar disc.

"For an enormous glory," he declared.

"No," she answered curtly. "For nothing, and worse than nothing. Destruction of everything I have lived for. Eternal loss to the heritage."

"Why, is not Earth the heritage?"

"No. Knowledge is. I tried to make that clear to Alpha." She paused. "To you I say again, the evolution of life, its adaptations, struggles, transformations, and how at last it meets death—those are unforeseeable, and nowhere else in the space-time universe can there be a world like this for them to play themselves out. They will enlighten us in ways the galactic brain itself cannot yet conceive. They may well open to us whole new phases of ultimate reality."

"Why would not a life that went on for gigayears do so, and more?"

"Because here I, the observer of the ages, have gained some knowledge of *this* destiny, some oneness with it—" She sighed. "Oh, you do not understand. You refuse to."

"On the contrary," Wayfarer said, as softly as might be, "I hope to. Among the reasons I came is that we can communicate being to being, perhaps more fully than across light-years and certainly more quickly."

She was silent a while. When she spoke again, her tone had gone gentle. "More . . . intimately. Yes. Forgive my resentment. It was wrong of me. I will indeed do what I can to make you welcome and help you learn."

"Thank you, thank you," Wayfarer said happily. "And I will do what I can toward that end."

The sun went under the cloud deck. A crescent moon stood aloft. The wind blew a little stronger, a little chillier.

"But if we decide against saving Earth," Wayfarer asked, "if it is to go molten and formless, every trace of its history dissolved, will you not mourn?"

"The record I have guarded will stay safe," Gaia replied.

He grasped her meaning: the database of everything known about this world. It was here in her. Much was also stored elsewhere, but she held the entirety. As the sun became a devouring monster, she would remove her physical plant to the outer reaches of the system.

"But you have done more than passively preserve it, have you not?" he said.

"Yes, of course." How could an intelligence like hers have refrained? "I have considered the data, worked with them, evaluated them, tried to reconstruct the conditions that brought them about."

*And in the past thousands of years she has become ever more taciturn about that, too, or downright evasive,* he thought.

"You had immense gaps to fill in," he hinted.

"Inevitably. The past, also, is quantum probabilistic. By what roads, what means, did history come to us?"

"Therefore, you create various emulations, to see what they lead to. About this she had told scarcely anything.

"You knew that. I admit, since you force me, that besides trying to find what happened, I make worlds to show what *might* have happened."

He was briefly startled. He had not been deliberately trying to bring out any such confession. Then he realized that she had foreseen he was bound to catch scent of it, once they joined their minds in earnest.

"Why?" he asked.

"Why else but for a more complete understanding?"

In his inwardness, Wayfarer reflected: Yes, she had been here since the time of humanity. The embryo of her existed before Christian Brannock was born. Into the growing fullness of her had gone the mind-patterns of humans who chose not to go to the stars but to abide on old Earth. And the years went by in their tens of millions.

Naturally, she was fascinated by the past. She must do most of her living in it. Could that be why she was indifferent to the near future, or actually wanted catastrophe?

Somehow that thought did not feel right to him. Gaia was a mystery he must solve.

Cautiously, he ventured, "Then you act as a physicist might, tracing hypothetical configurations of the wave function through space-time—except that the subjects of your experiments are conscious."

"I do no wrong," she said. "Come with me into any of those worlds and see."

"Gladly," he agreed, unsure whether he lied. He mustered resolution. "Just the same, duty demands I conduct my own survey of the material environment."

"As you will. Let me help you prepare." She was quiet for a span. In this thin air, a human would have seen the first stars blink into the sight. "But I believe it will be by sharing the history of my stewardship that we truly come to know one another."

Storm-battered until men must work the pumps without cease, the *Gray Courser* limped eastward along the southern coast of an unknown land. Wind set that direction, for the huukin trailed after, so worn and starved that what remained of its strength must be reserved for sorest need. The shore rolled jewel-green, save where woods dappled it darker, toward a wall of gentle hills. All was thick with life, grazing herds, wings multitudinous overhead, but no voyager had set foot there. Surf dashed in such violence that Kalava was not certain a boat could live through it. Meanwhile they had caught but little rainwater, and what was in the butts had gotten low and foul.

He stood in the bows, peering ahead, Ilyandi at his side. Wind boomed and shrilled, colder than they were used to. Wrack flew beneath an overcast gone heavy. Waves ran high, gray-green, white-maned, foam blown off them in streaks. The ship rolled, pitched, and groaned.

Yet, they had seen the sky uncommonly often. Ilyandi believed that clouds—doubtless vapors sucked from the ground by heat, turning back to water as they rose, like steam from a kettle—formed less readily in this clime. Too eagerly at her instruments and reckonings to speak much, she had now at last given her news to the captain.

"Then you think you know where we are?" he asked hoarsely.

Her face, gaunt within the cowl of a sea-stained cloak, bore the least smile. "No. This country is as nameless to me as to you. But, yes, I do think I can say we are no more than fifty daymarches from Ulonai, and it may be as little as forty."

Kalava's fist smote the rail. "By Ruvio's ax! How I hoped for this!" The words tumbled from him. "It means the weather tossed us mainly back and forth between the two shorelines. We've not come unreturnably far. Every ship henceforward can have a better passage. See you, she can first go out to the Ending Islands and wait at ease for favoring winds. The skipper will know he'll make landfall. We'll have it worked out after a few more voyages, just what lodestone bearing will bring him to what place hereabouts."

"But anchorage?" she wondered.

He laughed, which he had not done for many days and nights. "As for that—"

A cry from the lookout at the masthead broke through. Down the length of the vessel men raised their eyes. Terror howled.

Afterward no two tongues bore the same tale. One said that a firebolt had pierced the upper clouds, trailing thunder. Another told of a sword as long as the hull, and blood carried on the gale of its flight. To a third it was a beast with jaws agape and three tails aflame. . . . Kalava remembered a spear among whirling rainbows. To him Ilyandi said, when they were briefly alone, that she thought of a shuttle now seen, now unseen as it wove a web on which stood writing she could not read. All witnesses agreed that it came from over the sea, sped on inland through heaven, and vanished behind the hills.

Men went mad. Some ran about screaming. Some wailed to their gods. Some cast themselves down on the deck and shivered, or drew into balls and squeezed their eyes shut. No hand at helm or pumps, the ship wallowed about, sails banging, adrift toward the surf, while water drained in through sprung seams and lapped higher in the bilge.

"Avast!" roared Kalava. He sprang down the foredeck ladder and went among the crew. "Be you men? Up on your feet or die!" With kicks and cuffs he drove them back to their duties. One yelled and drew a knife on him. He knocked the fellow senseless. Barely in time, *Gray Courser* came again under control. She was then too near shore to get the huukin harnessed. Kalava took the helm, wore ship, and clawed back to sea room.

Mutiny was all too likely, once the sailors regained a little courage. When Kalava could yield place to a halfway competent steersman, he sought Ilyandi and they talked a while in her cabin. Thereafter they returned to the foredeck and he shouted for attention. Standing side by side, they looked down on the faces, frightened or terrified or sullen, of the men who had no immediate tasks.

"Hear this," Kalava said into the wind. "Pass it on to the rest. I know you'd turn south this day if you had your wish. But you can't. We'd never make the crossing, the shape we're in. Which would you lief have, the chance of wealth and fame or the certainty of drowning? We've got to make repairs, we've got to restock, and *then* we can sail home, bringing wondrous news. When can we fix things up? Soon, I tell you, soon. I've been looking at the water. Look for yourselves. See how it's taking on more and more of a brown shade, and how bits of plant stuff float about on the waves. That means a river, a big river, emptying out somewhere nigh. And that means a harbor for us. As for the sight we saw, here's the Vilku, our lady Ilyandi, to speak about it."

The skythinker stepped forward. She had changed into a clean white robe with the emblems of her calling, and held a staff topped by a sigil. Though her voice was low, it carried.

"Yes, that was a fearsome sight. It lends truth to the old stories of things that appeared to mariners who ventured, or were blown, far north. But think. Those sailors did win home again. Those who did not must have perished of natural causes. For why would the gods or the demons sink some and not others?

"What we ourselves saw merely flashed overhead. Was it warning us off? No, because if it knew that much about us, it knew we cannot immediately turn back. Did it give us any heed at all? Quite possibly not. It was very strange, yes, but that does not mean it was any threat. The world is full of strangenesses. I could tell you of things seen on clear nights over the centuries, fiery streaks down the sky or stars with glowing tails. We of the Vilkui do not understand them, but neither do we fear them. We give them their due honor and respect, as signs from the gods."

She paused before finishing: "Moreover, in the secret annals of our order lie accounts of visions and wonders exceeding these. All folk know that from time to time the gods have given their word to certain holy men or women, for the guidance of the people. I may not tell how they manifest themselves, but I will say that this today was not wholly unlike.

"Let us therefore believe that the sign granted us is a good one."

She went on to a protective chant-spell and an invocation of the Powers. That heartened most of her listeners. They were, after all, in considerable awe of her.

Besides, the larger part of them had sailed with Kalava before and done well out of it. They bullied the rest into obedience.

"Dismissed," said the captain. "Come evening, you'll get a ration of liquor."

A weak cheer answered him. The ship fared onward.

Next morning they did indeed find a broad, sheltered bay, dun with silt. Hitching up the huukin, they went cautiously in until they spied the river foretold by Kalava. Accompanied by a few bold men, he took a boat ashore. Marshes, meadows, and woods all had signs of abundant game. Various plants were unfamiliar, but he recognized others, among them edible fruits and bulbs. "It is well," he said. "This land is ripe for our taking." No lightning bolt struck him down.

Having located a suitable spot, he rowed back to the ship, brought her in on the tide, and beached her. He could see that the water often rose higher yet, so he would be able to float her off again when she was ready. That would take time, but he felt no haste. Let his folk make proper camp, he thought, get rested and nourished, before they began work. Hooks, nets, and weirs would give rich catches. Several of the crew had hunting skills as well. He did himself.

His gaze roved upstream, toward the hills. Yes, presently he would lead a detachment to learn what lay beyond.

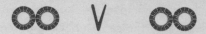

Gaia had never concealed her reconstructive research into human history. It was perhaps her finest achievement. But slowly those of her fellows in the galactic brain who paid close attention had come to feel that it was obsessing her. And then of late—within the past hundred thousand years or so—they were finding her reports increasingly scantier, less informative, at last ambiguous to the point of evasiveness. They did not press her about it; the patience of the universe was theirs. Nevertheless they had grown concerned. Especially had Alpha, who as the nearest was in the closest, most frequent contact; and therefore, now, had Wayfarer. Gaia's activities and attitudes were a primary factor in the destiny of Earth. Without a better understanding of her, the rightness of saving the planet was undecidable.

Surely an important part of her psyche was the history and archeology she preserved, everything from the animal origins to the machine fulfillment of genus Homo. Unnumbered individual minds had uploaded into her, too, had become elements of her being—far more than were in any other node. What had she made of all this over the megayears, and what had it made of her?

She could not well refuse Wayfarer admittance; the

heritage belonged to her entire fellowship, ultimately to intelligence throughout the cosmos of the future. Guided by her, he would go through the database of her observations and activities in external reality, geological, biological, astronomical.

As for the other reality, interior to her, the work she did with her records and emulations of humankind—to evaluate that, some purely human interaction seemed called for. Hence Wayfarer's makeup included the mind-pattern of a man.

Christian Brannock's had been chosen out of those whose uploads went starfaring because he was among the earliest, less molded than most by relationships with machines. Vigor, intelligence, and adaptability were other desired characteristics.

His personality was itself a construct, a painstaking refabrication by Alpha, who had taken strands (components, overtones) of his own mind and integrated them to form a consciousness that became an aspect of Wayfarer. No doubt it was not a perfect duplicate of the original. Certainly, while it had all the memories of Christian Brannock's lifetime, its outlook was that of a young man, not an old one. In addition, it possessed some knowledge—the barest sketch, grossly oversimplified so as not to overload it—of what had happened since its body died. Deep underneath its awareness lay the longing to return to an existence more full than it could now imagine. Yet, knowing that it would be taken back into the oneness when its task was done, it did not mourn any loss. Rather, to the extent that it was differentiated from Wayfarer, it took pleasure in sensations, thoughts, and emotions that it had effectively forgotten.

When the differentiation had been completed, the experience of being human again became well-nigh everything for it, and gladsome, because so had the man gone through life.

To describe how this was done, we must again resort to myth and say that Wayfarer downloaded the Christian Brannock subroutine into the main computer of the system that was Gaia. To describe what actually occurred would require the mathematics of wave mechanics and an entire concept of multi-leveled, mutably dimensioned reality that it had taken minds much greater than humankind's a long time to work out.

We can, however, try to make clear that what took place in the system was not a mere simulation. It was an emulation. Its events were not of a piece with events among the molecules of flesh and blood; but they were, in their way, just as real. The persons created had wills as free as any mortal's, and whatever dangers they met could do harm equal to anything a mortal body might suffer.

Consider a number of people at a given moment. Each is doing something, be it only thinking, remembering, or sleeping—together with all ongoing physiological and biochemical processes. They are interacting with each other and with their surroundings, too; and every element of these surroundings, be it only a stone or a leaf or a photon of sunlight, is equally involved. The complexity seems beyond conception, let alone enumeration or calculation. But consider further: At this one instant, every part of the whole, however minute, is in one specific state; and thus the whole itself is. Electrons are all in their particular quantum shells, atoms are all in their particular compounds and configurations, energy fields all have their particular values at each particular point—Suppose an infinitely fine-grained photograph.

A moment later, the state is different. However

slightly, fields have pulsed, atoms have shifted about, electrons have jumped, bodies have moved. But this new state derives from the first according to natural laws. And likewise for every succeeding state.

In crude, mythic language: Represent each variable of one state by some set of numbers; or, to put it in equivalent words, map the state into an $n$-dimensional phase space. Input the laws of nature. Run the program. The computer model should then evolve from state to state in exact correspondence with the evolution of our original matter-energy world. That includes life and consciousness. The maps of organisms go through one-to-one analogues of everything that the organisms themselves would, among these being the processes of sensation and thought. To them, they and their world are the same as in the original. The question of which set is the more real is meaningless.

Of course, this primitive account is false. The program did *not* exactly follow the course of events "outside." Gaia lacked both the data and the capability necessary to model the entire universe, or even the entire Earth. Likewise did any other node, and the galactic brain. Powers of that order lay immensely far in the future, if they would ever be realized. What Gaia could accommodate was so much less that the difference in degree amounted to a difference in kind.

For example, if events on the surface of a planet were to be played out, the stars must be lights in the night sky and nothing else, every other effect neglected. Only a limited locality on the globe could be done in anything like full detail; the rest grew more and more incomplete as distance from the scene increased, until at the antipodes there was little more than simplified geography, hydrography, and atmospherics. Hence weather on the scene would very soon be quite unlike weather at the corresponding moment of the original. This is the simplest, most obvious consequence of the limitations. The totality is beyond reckoning—and we have not even mentioned relativistic nonsimultaneity.

Besides, atom-by-atom modeling was a practical impossibility; statistical mechanics and approximations must substitute. Chaos and quantum uncertainties made developments incalculable in principle. Other, more profound considerations entered as well, but with them language fails utterly.

Let it be said, as a myth, that such creations made their destinies for themselves.

And yet, what a magnificent instrumentality the creator system was! Out of nothingness, it could bring worlds into being, evolutions, lives, ecologies, awarenesses, histories, entire timelines. They need not be fragmentary miscopies of something "real," dragging out their crippled spans until the nodal intelligence took pity and canceled them. Indeed, they need not derive in any way from the "outside." They could be works of imagination—fairy-tale worlds, perhaps, where benevolent gods ruled and magic ran free. Always, the logic of their boundary conditions caused them to develop appropriately, to be at home in their existences.

The creator system was the mightiest device ever made for the pursuit of art, science, philosophy, and understanding.

So it came about that Christian Brannock found himself alive again, young again, in the world that Gaia and Wayfarer had chosen for his new beginning.


2


He stood in a garden on a day of bright sun and mild, fragrant breezes. It was a formal garden, graveled paths, low-clipped hedges, roses and lilies in geometric beds, around a lichened stone basin where goldfish swam. Brick walls, ivy-heavy, enclosed three sides, a wrought-iron gate in them leading to a lawn. On the fourth side lay a house, white, slate-roofed, classically proportioned, a style that to him was antique. Honeybees buzzed. From a yew tree overlooking the wall came the twitter of birds.

A woman walked toward him. Her flower-patterned gown, the voluminous skirt and sleeves, a cameo hung on her bosom above the low neckline, dainty shoes, parasol less an accessory than a completion, made his twenty-third-century singlesuit feel abruptly barbaric. She was tall and well-formed. Despite the garments, her gait was lithe. As she neared, he saw clear features beneath high-piled mahogany hair.

She reached him, stopped, and met his gaze. "Benveni, Capita Brannock," she greeted. Her voice was low and musical.

"Uh, g'day, Sorita—uh—" he fumbled.

She blushed. "I beg your pardon, Captain Brannock. I forgot and used my Inglay—English of my time. I've been"—she hesitated—"supplied with yours, and we both have been with the contemporary language."

A sense of dream was upon him. To speak as dryly as he could was like clutching at something solid. "You're from my future, then?"

She nodded. "I was born about two hundred years after you."

"That means after my death, right?" He saw an inward shadow pass over her face. "I'm sorry," he blurted. "I didn't mean to upset you."

She turned entirely calm, even smiled a bit. "It's all right. We both know what we are, and what we used to be."

"But—"

"Yes, but." She shook her head. "It does feel strange, being . . . this . . . again."

He was quickly gaining assurance, settling into the situation. "I know. I've had practice in it," light-years away, at the star where Alpha dwelt. "Don't worry, it'll soon be quite natural to you."

"I have been here a little while myself. Nevertheless— Young," she whispered, "but remembering a long life, old age, dying—" She let the parasol fall, unnoticed, and stared down at her hands. Fingers gripped each other. "Remembering how toward the end I looked back and thought, 'Was that *all?* ' "

He wanted to take those hands in his and speak comfort, but decided he would be wiser to say merely, "Well, it wasn't all."

"No, of course not. Not for me, the way it had been once for everyone who ever lived. While my worn-out body was being painlessly terminated, my self-pattern was uploaded—" She raised her eyes. "Now we can't really recall what our condition has been like, can we?"

"We can look forward to returning to it."

"Oh, yes. Meanwhile—" She flexed herself, glanced about and upward, let light and air into her spirit, until at last a full smile blossomed. "I am starting to enjoy this. Already I am." She considered him. He was a tall man, muscular, blond, rugged of countenance. Laughter lines radiated from blue eyes. He spoke in a resonant baritone. "And I will."

He grinned, delighted. "Thanks. The same here. For openers, may I ask your name?"

"Forgive me!" she exclaimed. "I thought I was prepared. I . . . came into existence . . . with knowledge of my role and this milieu, and spent the time since rehearsing in my mind, but now that it's actually happened, all my careful plans have flown away. I am—was—no, I am Laurinda Ashcroft."

He offered his hand. After a moment she let him shake hers. He recalled that at the close of his mortal days the gesture was going out of use.

"You know a few things about me, I suppose," he said, "but I'm ignorant about you and your times. When I left Earth, everything was changing spinjump fast, and after that I was out of touch," and eventually his individuality went of its own desire into a greater one. This re-enactment of him had been given no details of the terrestrial history that followed his departure; it could not have contained any reasonable fraction of the information.

"You went to the stars almost immediately after you'd uploaded, didn't you?" she asked.

He nodded. "Why wait? I'd always longed to go."

"Are you glad that you did?"

"Glad is hardly the word." He spent two or three seconds putting phrases together. Language was important to him; he had been an engineer and occasionally a maker of songs. "However, I am also happy to be here." Again a brief grin. "In such pleasant company." Yet what he really hoped to do was explain himself. They would be faring together in search of one another's souls. "And I'll bring something new back to my proper existence. All at once I realize how a human can appreciate in a unique way what's out yonder," suns, worlds, upon certain of them life that was more wonderful still, nebular fire-clouds, infinity whirling down the throat of a black hole, galaxies like jewelwork strewn by a prodigal through immensity, space-time structure subtle and majestic—everything he had never known, as a man, until this moment, for no organic creature could travel those reaches.

"While I chose to remain on Earth," she said. "How timid and unimaginative do I seem to you?"

"Not in the least," he avowed. "You had the adventures you wanted."

"You are kind to say so." She paused. "Do you know Jane Austen?"

"Who? No, I don't believe I do."

"An early nineteenth-century writer. She led a quiet life, never went far from home, died young, but she explored people in ways that nobody else ever did."

"I'd like to read her. Maybe I'll get a chance here." He wished to show that he was no—"technoramus" was the word he invented on the spot. "I did read a good deal, especially on space missions. And especially poetry. Homer, Shakespeare, Tu Fu, Bashō, Bellman, Burns, Omar Khayyam, Kipling, Millay, Haldeman—" He threw up his hands and laughed. "Never mind. That's just the first several names I could grab out of the jumble for purposes of bragging."

"We have much getting acquainted to do, don't we? Come, I'm being inhospitable. Let's go inside, relax, and talk."

He retrieved her parasol for her and, recollecting historical dramas he had seen, offered her his arm. They walked slowly between the flowerbeds. Wind lulled, a bird whistled, sunlight baked odors out of the roses.

"Where are we?" he asked.

"And when?" she replied. "In England of the mid-eighteenth century, on an estate in Surrey." He nodded. He had in fact read rather widely. She fell silent, thinking, before she went on: "Gaia and Wayfarer decided a serene enclave like this would be the best rendezvous for us."

"Really? I'm afraid I'm as out of place as a toad on a keyboard."

She smiled, then continued seriously: "I told you I've been given familiarity with the milieu. We'll be visiting alien ones—whatever ones you choose, after I've explained what else I know about what she has been doing these many years. That isn't much. I haven't seen any other worlds of hers. You will take the leadership."

"You mean because I'm used to odd environments and rough people? Not necessarily. I dealt with nature, you know, on Earth and in space. Peaceful."

"Dangerous."

"Maybe. But never malign."

"Tell me," she invited.

They entered the house and seated themselves in its parlor. Casement windows stood open to green parkscape where deer grazed; afar were a thatched farm cottage, its outbuildings, and the edge of grainfields. Cleanly shaped furniture stood among paintings, etchings, books, two portrait busts. A maidservant rustled in with a tray of tea and cakes. She was obviously shocked by the newcomer but struggled to conceal it. When she had left, Laurinda explained to Christian that the owners of this place, Londoners to whom it was a summer retreat, had lent it to their friend, the eccentric Miss Ashcroft, for a holiday.

So had circumstances and memories been adjusted. It was an instance of Gaia directly interfering with the circumstances and events in an emulation. Christian wondered how frequently she did.

"Eccentricity is almost expected in the upper classes," Laurinda said. "But when you lived you could simply be yourself, couldn't you?"

In the hour that followed, she drew him out. His birth home was the Yukon Ethnate in the Bering Federation, and to it he often returned while he lived, for its wilderness preserves, mountain solitudes, and uncrowded, uncowed, plain-spoken folk. Otherwise, the nation was prosperous and progressive, with more connections to Asia and the Pacific than to the decayed successor states East and South. Across the Pole, it was also becoming intimate with the renascent societies of Europe, and there Christian received part of his education and spent a considerable amount of his free time.

His was an era of savage contrasts, in which the Commonwealth of Nations maintained a precarious peace. During a youthful, impulsively taken hitch in the Conflict Mediation Service, he twice saw combat. Later in his life, stability gradually became the norm. That was largely due to the growing influence of the artificial intelligence network. Most of its consciousness-level units interlinked in protean fashion to form minds appropriate for any particular situation, and already the capabilities of those minds exceeded the human. However, there was little sense of rivalry. Rather, there was partnership. The new minds were willing to advise, but were not interested in dominance.

Christian, child of forests and seas and uplands, heir to ancient civilizations, raised among their ongoing achievements, returned on his vacations to Earth in homecoming. Here were his kin, his friends, woods to roam, boats to sail, girls to kiss, songs to sing and glasses to raise (and a gravesite to visit. He barely mentioned his wife to Laurinda. She died before uploading technology was available). Always, though, he went back to space. It had called him since first he saw the stars from a cradle under the cedars. He became an engineer. Besides fellow humans he worked closely with sapient machines, and some of them got to be friends too, of an eerie kind. Over the decades, he took a foremost role in such undertakings as the domed Copernican Sea, the Asteroid Habitat, the orbiting antimatter plant, and finally the Grand Solar Laser for launching interstellar vessels on their way. Soon afterward, his body died, old and full of days; but the days of his mind had barely begun.

"A fabulous life," Laurinda said low. She gazed out over the land, across which shadows were lengthening. "I wonder if . . . they . . . might not have done better to give us a cabin in your wilderness."

"No, no," he said. "This is fresh and marvelous to me."

"We can easily go elsewhere, you know. Any place, any time that Gaia has generated, including ones that history never saw. I'll fetch our amulets whenever you wish."

He raised his brows. "Amulets?"

"You haven't been told—informed? They are devices. You wear yours and give it the command to transfer you."

He nodded. "I see. It maps an emulated person into different surroundings."

"With suitable modifications as required. Actually, in many cases it causes a milieu to be activated for you. Most have been in standby mode for a long time. I daresay Gaia could have arranged for us to wish ourselves to wherever we were going and call up whatever we needed likewise. But an external device is better."

He pondered. "Yes, I think I see why. If we got supernatural powers, we wouldn't really be human, would we? And the whole idea is that we should be." He leaned forward on his chair. "It's your turn. Tell me about yourself."

"Oh, there's too much. Not about me, I never did anything spectacular like you, but about the times I lived in, everything that happened to change this planet after you left it. . . ."

She was born here, in England. By then a thinly populated province of Europe, it was a quiet land ("half a-dream," she said) devoted to its memorials of the past. Not that creativity was dead; but the arts were rather sharply divided between ringing changes on classic works and efforts to deal with the revelations coming in from the stars. The esthetic that artificial intelligence was evolving for itself overshadowed both these schools. Nevertheless Laurinda was active in them.

Furthermore, in the course of her work she ranged widely over Earth. (By then, meaningful work for humans was a privilege that the talented and energetic strove to earn.) She was a liaison between the two kinds of beings. It meant getting to know people in their various societies and helping them make their desires count. For instance, a proposed earthquake control station would alter a landscape and disrupt a community; could it be resited, or if not, what cultural adjustments could be made? Most commonly, though, she counseled and aided individuals bewildered and spiritually lost.

Still more than him, she was carefully vague about her private life, but he got the impression that it was generally happy. If childlessness was an unvoiced sorrow, it was one she shared with many in a population-regulated world; he had had only a son. She loved Earth, its glories and memories, and every fine creation of her race. At the end of her mortality she chose to abide on the planet, in the wholeness that was to become Gaia.

He thought he saw why she had been picked for resurrection, to be his companion, out of all the uncounted millions who had elected the same destiny.

Aloud, he said, "Yes, this house is right for you. And me, in spite of everything. We're both of us more at home here than either of us could be in the other's native period. Peace and beauty."

"It isn't a paradise," she answered gravely. "This is the real eighteenth century, remember, as well as Gaia could reconstruct the history that led to it," always monitoring, making changes as events turned incompatible with what was in the chronicles and the archeology. "The household staff are underpaid, undernourished, underrespected—servile. The American colonists keep slaves and are going to rebel. Across the Channel, a rotted monarchy bleeds France white, and this will bring on a truly terrible revolution, followed by a quarter century of war."

He shrugged. "Well, the human condition never did include sanity, did it?" That was for the machines.

"In a few of our kind, it did," she said. "At least, they came close. Gaia thinks you should meet some, so you'll realize she isn't just playing cruel games. I have"—in the memories with which she had come into this being— "invited three for dinner tomorrow. It tampers a trifle with their actual biographies, but Gaia can remedy that later if she chooses." Laurinda smiled. "We'll have to make an amulet provide you with proper small clothes and wig."

"And you provide me with a massive briefing, I'm sure. Who are they?"

"James Cook, Henry Fielding, and Erasmus Darwin. I think it will be a lively evening."

The navigator, the writer, the polymath, three tiny, brilliant facets of the heritage that Gaia guarded.

## ∞ VI ∞

Now Wayfarer downloaded another secondary personality and prepared it to go survey Earth.

He, his primary self, would stay on the mountain, in a linkage with Gaia more close and complete than was possible over interstellar distances. She had promised to conduct him through her entire database of observations made across the entire planet during manifold millions of years. Even for those two, the undertaking was colossal. At the speed of their thought, it would take weeks of external time and nearly total concentration. Only a fraction of their awarenesses would remain available for anything else—a fraction smaller in him than in her, because her intellect was so much greater.

She told him of her hope that by this sharing, this virtually direct exposure to all she had perceived, he would come to appreciate why Earth should be left to its fiery doom. More was involved than scientific knowledge attainable in no other way. The events themselves would deepen and enlighten the galactic brain, as a great drama or symphony once did for humans. But Wayfarer must undergo their gigantic sweep through the past before he could feel the truth of what she said about the future.

He had his doubts. He wondered if her human components, more than had gone into any other node, might not have given her emotions, intensified by ages of brooding, that skewed her rationality. However, he consented to her proposal. It accorded with his purpose in coming here.

While he was thus engaged, Christian would be exploring her worlds of history and of might-have-been and a different agent would range around the physical, present-day globe.

In the latter case, his most obvious procedure was to discharge an appropriate set of the molecular assemblers he had brought along and let them multiply. When their numbers were sufficient, they would build (grow; brew) a fleet of miniature robotic vessels, which would fly about and transmit to him, for study at his leisure, everything their sensors detected.

Gaia persuaded him otherwise: "If you go in person, with a minor aspect of me for a guide, you will get to know the planet more quickly and thoroughly. Much about it is unparalleled. It may help you see why I want the evolution to continue unmolested to its natural conclusion."

He accepted. After all, a major part of his mission was to fathom her thinking. Then perhaps Alpha and the rest could hold a true dialogue with her and reach an agreement—whatever it was going to be. Besides, he could deploy his investigators later if this expedition left him dissatisfied.

He did inquire: "What are the hazards?"

"Chiefly weather," she admitted. "With conditions growing more extreme, tremendous storms spring up practically without warning. Rapid erosion can change contours almost overnight, bringing landslides, flash floods, sudden emergence of tidal bores. I do not attempt to monitor in close detail. That volume of data would be more than I could handle"—yes, she—"when my main concern is the biological phenomena."

His mind reviewed her most recent accounts to the stars. They were grim. The posthuman lushness of nature was megayears gone. Under its clouds, Earth roasted. The loftiest mountaintops were bleak, as here above the Rainbowl, but nothing of ice or snow remained except dim geological traces. Apart from the waters and a few islands where small, primitive species hung on, the tropics were sterile deserts. Dust and sand borne on furnace winds scoured their rockscapes. North and south they encroached, withering the steppes, parching the valleys, crawling up into the hills. Here and there survived a jungle or a swamp, lashed by torrential rains or wrapped hot and sullen in fog, but it would not be for much longer. Only in the high latitudes did a measure of benignity endure. Arctica's climates ranged from Floridian—Christian Brannock's recollections—to cold on the interior heights. South of it across a sea lay a broad continent whose northerly parts had temperatures reminiscent of central Africa. Those were the last regions where life kept any abundance.

"Would you really not care to see a restoration?" Wayfarer had asked her directly, early on.

"Old Earth lives in my database and emulations," Gaia had responded. "I could not map this that is happening into those systems and let it play itself out, because I do not comprehend it well enough, nor can any finite mind. To divert the course of events would be to lose, forever, knowledge that I feel will prove to be of fundamental importance."

Wayfarer had refrained from pointing out that life, reconquering a world once more hospitable to it, would not follow predictable paths either. He knew she would retort that experiments of that kind were being conducted on a number of formerly barren spheres, seeded with synthesized organisms. It had seemed strange to him that she appeared to lack any sentiment about the mother of humankind. Her being included the beings of many and many a one who had known sunrise dew beneath a bare foot, murmurs in forest shades, wind-waves in wheatfields from horizon to horizon, yes, and the lights and clangor of great cities. It was, at root, affection, more than any scientific or technological challenge, that had roused in Gaia's fellows among the stars the wish to make Earth young again.

Now she meant to show him why she felt that death should have its way.

Before entering rapport with her, he made ready for his expedition. Gaia offered him an aircraft, swift, versatile, able to land on a square meter while disturbing scarcely a leaf. He supplied a passenger for it.

He had brought along several bodies of different types. The one he picked would have to operate independently of him, with a separate intelligence. Gaia could spare a minim of her attention to have telecommand of the flyer; he could spare none for his representative, if he was to range through the history of the globe with her.

The machine he picked was not equivalent to him. Its structure could never have supported a matrix big enough to operate at his level of mentality. Think of it, metaphorically, as possessing a brain equal to that of a high-order human. Into this brain had been copied as much of Wayfarer's self-pattern as it could hold—the merest sketch, a general idea of the situation, incomplete and distorted like this myth of ours. However, it had reserves it could call upon. Inevitably, because of being the most suitable, the Christian Brannock aspect dominated.

So you may, if you like, think of the man as being

reborn in a body of metal, silicates, carbon and other compounds, electricity and other forces, photon and particle exchanges, quantum currents. It was not quite the same as his earlier postmortal robotic existence. There was more richness, even more passion, though his passions were not identical with those of flesh. In most respects, he differed more from the long-dead mortal than did the re-creation in Gaia's emulated worlds. If we call the latter Christian, we can refer to the former as Brannock.

His frame was of approximately human size and shape. Matte blue-gray, it had four arms. He could reshape the hands of the lower pair as desired, to be a tool kit. He could similarly adapt his feet according to the demands upon them, and could extrude a spindly third leg for support or extra grip. His back swelled outward to hold a nuclear energy source and various organs. His head was a domed cylinder. The sensors in it and throughout the rest of him were not conspicuous but gave him full-surround information. The face was a holographic screen in which he could generate whatever image he wished. Likewise could he produce every frequency of sound, plus visible light, infrared, and microwave radio, for sensing or for short-range communication. A memory unit, out of which he could quickly summon any data, was equivalent to a large ancient library.

He could not process those data, comprehend and reason about them, at higher speed than a human genius. He had other limitations as well. But then, he was never intended to function independently of equipment.

He was soon ready to depart. Imagine him saying to Wayfarer, with a phantom grin, "Adios. Wish me luck."

The response was . . . absent-minded. Wayfarer was beginning to engage with Gaia.

Thus Brannock boarded the aircraft in a kind of silence. To the eye it rested small, lanceolate, iridescently aquiver. The material component was a tissue of wisps. Most of that slight mass was devoted to generating forces and maintaining capabilities, which Gaia had not listed for him. Yet it would take a wind of uncommon violence to endanger this machine, and most likely it could outrun the menace.

He settled down inside. Wayfarer had insisted on manual controls, against emergencies that he conceded were improbable, and Gaia's effectors had made the modifications. An insubstantial configuration shimmered before Brannock, instruments to read, keypoints to touch or think at. He leaned back into a containing field and let her pilot. Noiselessly, the flyer ascended, then came down through the cloud deck and made a leisurely way at five hundred meters above the foothills.

"Follow the Remnant River to the sea," Brannock requested. "The view inbound was beautiful."

"As you like," said Gaia. They employed sonics, his voice masculine, hers—perhaps because she supposed he preferred it—feminine in a low register. Their conversation did not actually go as reported here. She changed course and he beheld the stream shining amidst the deep greens of the Bountiful Valley, under a silver-gray heaven. "The plan, you know, is that we shall cruise about Arctica first. I have an itinerary that should provide you a representative sampling of its biology. At our stops, you can investigate as intensively as you care to, and if you want to stop anyplace else we can do that too."

"Thank you," he said. "The idea is to furnish me a kind of baseline, right?"

"Yes, because conditions here are the easiest for life. When you are ready, we will proceed south, across lands increasingly harsh. You will learn about the adaptations life has made. Many are extraordinarily interesting. The galactic brain itself cannot match the creativity of nature."

"Well, sure. Chaos, complexity. . . . You've described quite a few of those adaptations to, uh, us, haven't you?"

"Yes, but by no means all. I keep discovering new ones. Life keeps evolving."

*As environments worsened,* Brannock thought. And nonetheless, species after species went extinct. He got a sense of a rear-guard battle against the armies of hell.

"I want you to experience this as fully as you are able," Gaia said, "immerse yourself, *feel* the sublimity of it."

*The tragedy,* he thought. But tragedy was art, maybe the highest art that humankind ever achieved. And more of the human soul might well linger in Gaia than in any of her fellow intelligences.

Had she kept a need for catharsis, for pity and terror? What really went on in her emulations?

Well, Christian was supposed to find out something about that. If he could.

Brannock was human enough himself to protest. He gestured at the land below, where the river flowed in its canyons through the coastal hills, to water a wealth of forest and meadow before emptying into a bay above which soared thousands of wings. "You want to watch the struggle till the end," he said. "Life wants to live. What right have you to set your wish against that?"

"The right of awareness," she declared. "Only to a being that is conscious do justice, mercy, desire have any existence, any meaning. Did not humans always use the world as they saw fit? When nature finally got protection, that was because humans so chose. I speak for the knowledge and insight that *we* can gain."

The question flickered uneasily in him: *What about her private emotional needs?*

Abruptly the aircraft veered. The turn pushed Brannock hard into the force field upholding him. He heard air crack and scream. The bay fell aft with mounting speed.

The spaceman in him, who had lived through meteoroid strikes and radiation bursts because he was quick, had already acted. Through the optical magnification he immediately ordered up, he looked back to see what the trouble was. The glimpse he got, before the sight went under the horizon, made him cry, "Yonder!"

"What?" Gaia replied as she hurtled onward.

"That back there. Why are you running from it?"

"What do you mean? There is nothing important."

"The devil there isn't. I've a notion you saw it more clearly than I did."

Gaia slowed the headlong flight until she well-nigh hovered above the strand and wild surf. He felt a sharp suspicion that she did it in order to dissipate the impression of urgency, make him more receptive to whatever she intended to claim.

"Very well," she said after a moment. "I spied a certain object. What do you think you saw?"

He decided not to answer straightforwardly—at least, not before she convinced him of her good faith. The more information she had, the more readily she could contrive a deception. Even this fragment of her intellect was superior to his. Yet he had his own measure of wits, and an ingrained stubbornness.

"I'm not sure, except that it didn't seem dangerous. Suppose you tell me what it is and why you turned tail from it."

Did she sigh? "At this stage of your knowledge, you

would not understand. Rather, you would be bound to misunderstand. That is why I retreated."

A human would have tensed every muscle. Brannock's systems went on full standby. "I'll be the judge of my brain's range, if you please. Kindly go back."

"No. I promise I will explain later, when you have seen enough more."

Seen enough illusions? She might well have many trickeries waiting for him. "As you like," Brannock said. "Meanwhile, I'll give Wayfarer a call and let him know." Alpha's emissary kept a minute part of his sensibility open to outside stimuli.

"No, do not," Gaia said. "It would distract him unnecessarily."

"He will decide that," Brannock told her.

Strife exploded.

Almost, Gaia won. Had her entirety been focused on attack, she would have carried it off with such swiftness that Brannock would never have known he was bestormed. But a fraction of her was dealing, as always, with her observing units around the globe and their torrents of data. Possibly it also glanced from time to time—through the quantum shifts inside her—at the doings of Christian and Laurinda. By far the most of her was occupied in her interaction with Wayfarer. This she could not set aside without rousing instant suspicion. Rather, she must make a supremely clever effort to conceal from him that anything untoward was going on.

Moreover, she had never encountered a being like Brannock, human male aggressiveness and human spacefarer's reflexes blent with sophisticated technology and something of Alpha's immortal purpose.

He felt the support field strengthen and tighten to hold him immobile. He felt a tide like delirium rush into his mind. A man would have thought it was a knockout anesthetic. Brannock did not stop to wonder. He reacted directly, even as she struck. Machine fast and tiger ferocious, he put her off balance for a crucial millisecond.

Through the darkness and roaring in his head, he lashed out physically. His hands tore through the light-play of control nexuses before him. They were not meant to withstand an assault. He could not seize command, but he could, blindly, disrupt.

Arcs leaped blue-white. Luminances flared and died. Power output continued; the aircraft stayed aloft. Its more complex functions were in ruin. Their dance of atoms, energies, and waves went uselessly random.

The bonds that had been closing on Brannock let go. He sagged to the floor. The night in his head receded. It left him shaken, his senses awhirl. Into the sudden anarchy of everything he yelled, "Stop, you bitch!"

"I will," Gaia said.

Afterward he realized that she had kept a vestige of governance over the flyer. Before he could wrest it from her, she sent them plunging downward and cut off the main generator. Every force field blinked out. Wind ripped the material frame asunder. Its pieces crashed in the surf. Combers tumbled them about, cast a few on the beach, gave the rest to the undertow.

As the craft fell, disintegrating, Brannock gathered his strength and leaped. The thrust of his legs cast him outward, through a long arc that ended in deeper water. It fountained high and white when he struck. He went down into green depths while the currents swept him to and fro. But he hit the sandy bottom unharmed.

Having no need to breathe, he stayed under. To recover from the shock took him less than a second. To make his assessment took minutes, there in the swirling surges.

Gaia had tried to take him over. A force field had begun to damp the processes in his brain and impose its own patterns. He had quenched it barely in time.

She would scarcely have required a capability of that kind in the past. Therefore she had invented and installed it specifically for him. This strongly suggested she had meant to use it at some point of their journey. When he saw a thing she had not known was there and refused to be fobbed off, he compelled her to make the attempt before she was ready. When it failed, she spent her last resources to destroy him.

She would go that far, that desperately, to keep a secret that tremendous from the stars.

He recognized a mistake in his thinking. She had not used up everything at her beck. On the contrary, she had a planetful of observers and other instrumentalities to call upon. Certain of them must be bound here at top speed, to make sure he was dead—or, if he lived, to make sure of him. Afterward she would feed Wayfarer a story that ended with a regrettable accident away off over an ocean.

Heavier than water, Brannock strode down a sloping sea floor in search of depth.

Having found a jumble of volcanic rock, he crawled into a lava tube, lay fetally curled, and willed his systems to operate as low-level as might be. He hoped that then her agents would miss him. Neither their numbers nor their sensitivities were infinite. It would be reasonable for Gaia—who could not have witnessed his escape, her sensors in the aircraft being obliterated as it came apart—to conclude that the flows had taken his scattered remains away.

## 2

After three days and nights, the internal clock he had set brought him back awake.

He knew he must stay careful. However, unless she kept a closer watch on the site than he expected she would—for Wayfarer, in communion with her, might too readily notice that she was concentrating on one little patch of the planet—he dared now move about. His electronic senses ought to warn him of any robot that came into his vicinity, even if it was too small for eyes to see. Whether he could then do anything about it was a separate question.

First he searched the immediate area. Gaia's machines had removed those shards of the wreck that they found, but most were strewn over the bottom, and she had evidently not thought it worthwhile, or safe, to have them sought out. Nearly all of what he came upon was in fact scrap. A few units were intact. The one that interested him had the physical form of a small metal sphere. He tracked it down by magnetic induction. Having taken it to a place ashore, hidden by trees from the sky, he studied it. With his tool-hands he traced the (mythic) circuitry within and identified it as a memory bank. The encoding was familiar to his Wayfarer aspect. He extracted the information and stored it in his own database.

A set of languages. Human languages, although none he had ever heard of. Yes, very interesting.

"I'd better get hold of those people," he muttered. In the solitude of wind, sea, and wilderness, he had relapsed into an ancient habit of occasionally thinking aloud. "Won't likely be another chance. Quite a piece of news for Wayfarer." If he came back, or at least got within range of his transmitter.

He set forth afoot, along the shore toward the bay where the Remnant River debouched. Maybe that which he had seen would be there yet, or traces of it.

He wasn't sure, everything had happened so fast, but he thought it was a ship.

Three days—olden Earth days of twenty-four hours, cool sunlight, now and then a rain shower leaving pastures and hedgerows asparkle, rides through English lanes, rambles through English towns, encounters with folk, evensong in a Norman church, exploration of buildings and books, long talks and companionable silences—wrought friendship. In Christian it also began to rouse kindlier feelings toward Gaia. She had resurrected Laurinda, and Laurinda was a part of her, as he was of Wayfarer and of Alpha and more other minds across the galaxy than he could number. Could the rest of Gaia's works be wrongful?

No doubt, she had chosen and planned as she did in order to get this reaction from him. It didn't seem to matter.

Nor did the primitive conditions of the eighteenth century matter to him or to Laurinda. Rather, their everyday experiences were something refreshingly new, and frequently the occasion of laughter. What did become a bit difficult for him was to retire decorously to his separate room each night.

But they had their missions: his to see what was going on in this reality and afterward upload into Wayfarer; hers to explain and justify it to him as well as a mortal was able. Like him, she kept a memory of having been one with a nodal being. The memory was as dim and fragmentary as his, more a sense of transcendence than anything with a name or form, like the afterglow of a religious vision long ago. Yet it pervaded her personality, the unconscious more than the conscious; and it was her relationship to Gaia, as he had his to Wayfarer and beyond that to Alpha. In a limited, mortal, but altogether honest and natural way, she spoke for the node of Earth.

By tacit consent, they said little about the purpose and simply enjoyed their surroundings and one another, until the fourth morning. Perhaps the weather whipped up a lifetime habit of duty. Wind gusted and shrilled around the house, rain blinded the windows, there would be no going out even in a carriage. Indoors a fire failed to hold dank chill at bay. Candlelight glowed cozily on the breakfast table, silverware and china sheened, but shadows hunched thick in every corner.

He took a last sip of coffee, put the cup down, and ended the words he had been setting forth: "Yes, we'd better get started. Not that I've any clear notion of what to look for. Wayfarer himself doesn't." Gaia had been so vague about so much. Well, Wayfarer was now (whatever "now" meant) in rapport with her, seeking an overall, cosmic view of—how many millions of years on this planet?

"Why, you know your task," Laurinda replied. "You're to find out the nature of Gaia's interior activity, what it means in moral—in human terms." She straightened in her chair. Her tone went resolute. "We *are* human, we emulations. We think and act, we feel joy and pain, the same as humans always did."

Impulse beckoned; it was his wont to try to lighten

moods. "And," he added, "make new generations of people, the same as humans always did."

A blush crossed the fair countenance. "Yes," she said. Quickly: "Of course, most of what's . . . here . . . is nothing but database. Archives, if you will. We might start by visiting one or two of those reconstructions."

He smiled, the heaviness lifting from him. "I'd love to. Any suggestions?"

Eagerness responded. "The Acropolis of Athens? As it was when new? Classical civilization fascinated me." She tossed her head. "Still does, by damn."

"Hm." He rubbed his chin. "From what I learned in my day, those old Greeks were as tricky, quarrelsome, short-sighted a pack of political animals as ever stole an election or bullied a weaker neighbor. Didn't Athens finance the building of the Parthenon by misappropriating the treasury of the Delian League?"

"They were human," she said, almost too low for him to hear above the storm-noise. "But what they made—"

"Sure," he answered. "Agreed. Let's go."


2


In perception, the amulets were silvery two-centimeter discs that hung on a user's breast, below garments. In reality—outer-viewpoint reality—they were powerful, subtle programs with intelligences of their own. Christian wondered about the extent to which they were under the direct control of Gaia, and how closely she was monitoring him.

Without thinking, he took Laurinda's hand. Her fingers clung to his. She looked straight before her, though, into the flickery fire, while she uttered their command.

## 3

Immediately, with no least sensation of movement, they were on broad marble steps between outworks, under a cloudless heaven, in flooding hot radiance. From the steepest, unused hill slopes, a scent of wild thyme drifted up through silence, thyme that had had no bees to quicken it or hands to pluck it. Below reached the city, sun-smitten houseroofs, open agoras, colonnaded temples. In this clear air Christian imagined he could well-nigh make out the features on the statues.

After a time beyond time, the visitors moved upward, still mute, still hand in hand, to where winged Victories lined the balustrade before the sanctuary of Nike Apteros. Their draperies flowed to movement he did not see and wind he did not feel. One was tying her sandals. . . .

For a long while the two lingered at the Propylaea, its porticos, Ionics, Dorics, paintings, votive tablets in the Pinakotheka. They felt they could have stayed past sunset, but everything else awaited them, and they knew mortal enthusiasm as they would presently know mortal weariness. Colors burned. . . .

The stone flowers and stone maidens at the Erechtheum. . . .

Christian had thought of the Parthenon as exquisite; so it was in the pictures and models he had seen, while the broken, chemically gnawed remnants under shelter were merely to grieve over. Confronting it here, entering it, he discovered its sheer size and mass. Life shouted in the friezes, red, blue, gilt; then in the dusk within, awesomeness and beauty found their focus in the colossal Athene of Pheidias.

—Long afterward, he stood with Laurinda on the Wall of Kimon, above the Asclepium and Theater of Dionysus. A westering sun made the city below intricate with shadows, and coolth breathed out of the east. Hitherto, when they spoke it had been, illogically, in near whispers. Now they felt free to talk openly, or did they feel a need?

He shook his head. "Gorgeous," he said, for lack of anything halfway adequate. "Unbelievable."

"It was worth all the wrongdoing and war and agony," she murmured. "Wasn't it?"

For the moment, he shied away from deep seriousness. "I didn't expect it to be this, uh, gaudy—no, this bright."

"They painted their buildings. That's known."

"Yes, I knew too. But were later scholars sure of just what colors?"

"Scarcely, except where a few traces were left. Most of this must be Gaia's conjecture. The sculpture especially, I suppose. Recorded history saved only the barest description of the Athene, for instance." Laurinda paused. Her gaze went outward to the mountains. "But surely this—in view of everything she has, all the information, and being able to handle it all at once and, and understand the minds that were capable of making it— surely this is the most likely reconstruction. Or the least unlikely."

"She may have tried variations. Would you like to go see?"

"No, I, I think not, unless you want to. This has been overwhelming, hasn't it?" She hesitated. "Besides, well—"

He nodded. "Yeh." With a gesture at the soundless, motionless, smokeless city below and halidoms around:

"Spooky. At best, a museum exhibit. Not much to our purpose, I'm afraid."

She met his eyes. "Your purpose. I'm only a—not even a guide, really. Gaia's voice to you? No, just a, an undertone of her, if that." The smile that touched her lips was somehow forlorn. "I suspect my main reason for existing again is to keep you company."

He laughed and offered her a hand, which for a moment she clasped tightly. "I'm very glad of the company, eccentric Miss Ashcroft."

Her smile warmed and widened. "Thank you, kind sir. And I am glad to be . . . alive . . . today. What should we do next?"

"Visit some living history, I think," he said. "Why not Hellenic?"

She struck her palms together. "The age of Pericles!"

He frowned. "Well, I don't know about that. The Peloponnesian War, the plague—and foreigners like us, barbarians, you a woman, we wouldn't be too well received, would we?"

He heard how she put disappointment aside and looked forward anew. "When and where, then?"

"Aristotle's time? If I remember rightly, Greece was peaceful then, no matter how much hell Alexander was raising abroad, and the society was getting quite cosmopolitan. Less patriarchal, too. Anyhow, Aristotle's always interested me. In a way, he was one of the earliest scientists."

"We had better inquire first. But before that, let's go home to a nice hot cup of tea!"

# 4

They returned to the house at the same moment as they left it, to avoid perturbing the servants. There they found that lack of privacy joined with exhaustion to keep them from speaking of anything other than trivia. However, that was all right; they were good talkmates.

The next morning, which was brilliant, they went out into the garden and settled on a bench by the fish basin. Drops of rain glistened on flowers, whose fragrance awoke with the strengthening sunshine. No one else was in sight or earshot. This time Christian addressed the amulets. His felt suddenly heavy around his neck, and the words came out awkwardly. He need not have said them aloud, but it helped him give shape to his ideas.

The reply entered directly into their brains. He rendered it to himself, irrationally, as in a dry, professorish tenor:

"Only a single Hellenic milieu has been carried through many generations. It includes the period you have in mind. It commenced at the point of approximately 500 B.C.E., with an emulation as historically accurate as possible."

*But nearly everyone then alive was lost to history,* thought Christian. Except for the few who were in the chronicles, the whole population must needs be created out of Gaia's imagination, guided by knowledge and logic; and those few named persons were themselves almost entirely new-made, their very DNA arbitrarily laid out.

"The sequence was revised as necessary," the amulet continued.

*Left to itself, that history would soon have drifted completely away from the documents, and eventually from the archeology,* Christian thought. *Gaia saw this start to happen, over and over. She rewrote the program—events, memories, personalities, bodies, births, lifespans, deaths—and let it resume until it deviated again. Over and over.* The morning felt abruptly cold.

"Much was learned on every such occasion," said the amulet. "The situation appeared satisfactory by the time

Macedonian hegemony was inevitable, and thereafter the sequence was left to play itself out undisturbed. Naturally, it still did not proceed identically with the historical past. Neither Aristotle nor Alexander was born. Instead, a reasonably realistic conqueror lived to a ripe age and bequeathed a reasonably well-constructed empire. He did have a Greek teacher in his youth, who had been a disciple of Plato."

"Who was that?" Christian asked out of a throat gone dry.

"His name was Eumenes. In many respects he was equivalent to Aristotle, but had a more strongly empirical orientation. This was planned."

*Eumenes was specially ordained, then. Why?*

"If we appear and meet him, w-won't that change what comes after?"

"Probably not to any significant extent. Or if it does, that will not matter. The original sequence is in Gaia's database. Your visit will, in effect, be a reactivation."

"Not one for your purpose," Laurinda whispered into the air. "What was it? What happened in that world?"

"The objective was experimental, to study the possible engendering of a scientific-technological revolution analogous to that of the seventeenth century C.E., with accompanying social developments that might foster the evolution of a stable democracy."

Christian told himself furiously to pull out of his funk. "Did it?" he challenged.

The reply was calm. "Do you wish to study it?"

Christian had not expected any need to muster his courage. After a minute he said, word by slow word, "Yes, I think that might be more useful than meeting your philosopher. Can you show us the outcome of the experiment?"

Laurinda joined in: "Oh, I know there can't be any

single, simple picture. But can you bring us to a, a scene that will give an impression—a kind of epitome—like, oh, King John at Runnymede or Elizabeth the First knighting Francis Drake or Einstein and Bohr talking about the state of their world?"

"An extreme possibility occurs in a year corresponding to your 894 C.E.," the amulet told him. "I suggest Athens as the locale. Be warned, it is dangerous. I can protect you, or remove you, but human affairs are inherently chaotic and this situation is more unpredictable than most. It could escape my control."

"I'll go," Christian snapped.

"And I," Laurinda said.

He glared at her. "No. You heard. It's dangerous."

Gone quite calm, she stated, "It is necessary for me. Remember, I travel on behalf of Gaia."

Gaia, who let the thing come to pass.

# 5

Transfer.

For an instant, they glanced at themselves. They had known the amulets would convert their garb to something appropriate. She wore a gray gown, belted, reaching halfway down her calves, with shoes, stockings, and a scarf over hair coiled in braids. He was in tunic, trousers, and boots of the same coarse materials, a sheath knife at his hip and a long-barreled firearm slung over his back.

Their surroundings smote them. They stood in a Propylaea that was scarcely more than tumbled stones and snags of sculpture. The Parthenon was not so shattered, but scarred, weathered, here and there buttressed with brickwork from which thrust the mouths of rusted cannon. All else was ruin. The Erechtheum looked as if it had been quarried. Below them, the city burned. They could see little of it through smoke that stained the sky and savaged their nostrils. A roar of conflagration reached them, and bursts of gunfire.

A woman came running out of the haze, up the great staircase. She was young, dark-haired, unkempt, ragged, begrimed, desperate. A man came after, a burly blond in a fur cap, dirty red coat, and leather breeches. Beneath a sweeping mustache, he leered. He too was armed, murderously big knife, firearm in right hand.

The woman saw Christian looming before her. *"Voetho!"* she screamed. *"Onome Theou, kyrie, voetho!"* She caught her foot against a step and fell. Her pursuer stopped before she could rise and stamped a boot down on her back.

Through his amulet, Christian understood the cry. "Help, in God's name, sir, help!" Fleetingly he thought the language must be a debased Greek. The other man snarled at him and brought weapon to shoulder.

Christian had no time to unlimber his. While the stranger was in motion, he bent, snatched up a rock— a fragment of a marble head—and cast. It thudded against the stranger's nose. He lurched back, his face a sudden red grotesque. His gun clattered to the stairs. He howled.

With the quickness that was his in emergencies, Christian rejected grabbing his own firearm. He had seen that its lock was of peculiar design. He might not be able to discharge it fast enough. He drew his knife and lunged downward. "Get away, you swine, before I open your guts!" he shouted. The words came out in the woman's language.

The other man retched, turned, and staggered off. Well before he reached the bottom of the hill, smoke had swallowed sight of him. Christian halted at the woman's huddled form and sheathed his blade. "Here, sister," he said, offering his hand, "come along. Let's get to shelter. There may be more of them."

She crawled to her feet, gasping, leaned heavily on his arm, and limped beside him up to the broken gateway. Her features Mediterranean, she was doubtless a native. She looked half starved. Laurinda came to her other side. Between them, the visitors got her into the portico of the Parthenon. Beyond a smashed door lay an interior dark and empty of everything but litter. It would be defensible if necessary.

An afterthought made Christian swear at himself. He went back for the enemy's weapon. When he returned, Laurinda sat with her arms around the woman, crooning comfort. "There, darling, there, you're safe with us. Don't be afraid. We'll take care of you."

The fugitive lifted big eyes full of night. "Are . . . you . . . angels from heaven?" she mumbled.

"No, only mortals like you," Laurinda answered through tears. That was not exactly true, Christian thought; but what else could she say? "We do not even know your name."

"I am . . . Zoe . . . Comnenaina—"

"Bone-dry, I hear from your voice." Laurinda lifted her head. Her lips moved in silent command. A jug appeared on the floor, bedewed with cold. "Here is water. Drink."

Zoe had not noticed the miracle. She snatched the vessel and drained it in gulp after gulp. When she was through she set it down and said, "Thank you," dully but with something of strength and reason again in her.

"Who was that after you?" Christian asked.

She drew knees to chin, hugged herself, stared before her, and replied in a dead voice, "A Flemic soldier. They broke into our house. I saw them stab my father. They laughed and laughed. I ran out the back and down the streets. I thought I could hide on the Acropolis. Nobody comes here anymore. That one saw me and came after. I suppose he would have killed me when he was done. That would have been better than if he took me away with him."

Laurinda nodded. "An invading army," she said as tonelessly. "They took the city and now they are sacking it."

Christian thumped the butt of his gun down on the stones. "Does Gaia let this go *on?*" he grated.

Laurinda lifted her gaze to his. It pleaded. "She must. Humans must have free will. Otherwise they're puppets."

"But how did they get into this mess?" Christian demanded. "Explain it if you can!"

The amulet(s) replied with the same impersonality as before:

"The Hellenistic era developed scientific method. This, together with the expansion of commerce and geographical knowledge, produced an industrial revolution and parliamentary democracy. However, neither the science nor the technology progressed beyond an approximate equivalent of your eighteenth century. Unwise social and fiscal policies led to breakdown, dictatorship, and repeated warfare."

Christian's grin bared teeth. "That sounds familiar."

"Alexander Tytler said it in our eighteenth century," Laurinda muttered unevenly. "No republic has long outlived the discovery by a majority of its people that they could vote themselves largesse from the public treasury." Aloud: "Christian, they were only human."

Zoe hunched lost in her sorrow.

"You oversimplify," stated the amulet voice. "But this

is not a history lesson. To continue the outline, inevitably engineering information spread to the warlike barbarians of northern Europe and western Asia. If you question why they were granted existence, reflect that a population confined to the littoral of an inland sea could not model any possible material world. The broken-down societies of the South were unable to change their characters, or prevail over them, or eventually hold them off. The end results are typified by what you see around you."

"The Dark Ages," Christian said dully. "What happens after them? What kind of new civilization?"

"None. This sequence terminates in one more of its years."

"Huh?" he gasped. "Destroyed?"

"No. The program ceases to run. The emulation stops."

"My God! Those millions of lives—as real as, as mine—"

Laurinda stood up and held her arms out into the fouled air. "Does Gaia know, then, does Gaia know this time line would never get any happier?" she cried.

"No," said the voice in their brains. "Doubtless the potential of further progress exists. However, you forget that while Gaia's capacities are large, they are not infinite. The more attention she devotes to one history, the details of its planet as well as the length of its course, the less she has to give to others. The probability is too small that this sequence will lead to a genuinely new form of society."

Slowly, Laurinda nodded. "I see."

"I don't," Christian snapped. "Except that Gaia's inhuman."

Laurinda shook her head and laid a hand on his. "No, not that. Posthuman. *We* built the first artificial intelligences." After a moment: "Gaia isn't cruel. The universe often is, and she didn't create it. She's seeking something better than blind chance can make."

"Maybe." His glance fell on Zoe. "Look, something's got to be done for this poor soul. Never mind if we change the history. It's due to finish soon anyway."

Laurinda swallowed and wiped her eyes. "Give her her last year in peace," she said into the air. "Please."

Objects appeared in the room behind the doorway. "Here are food, wine, clean water," said the unheard voice. "Advise her to return downhill after dark, find some friends, and lead them back. A small party, hiding in these ruins, can hope to survive until the invaders move on."

"It isn't worthwhile doing more, is it?" Christian said bitterly. "Not to you."

"Do you wish to end your investigation?"

"No, be damned if I will."

"Nor I," said Laurinda. "But when we're through here, when we've done the pitiful little we can for this girl, take us home."

# 6

Peace dwelt in England. Clouds towered huge and white, blue-shadowed from the sunlight spilling past them. Along the left side of a lane, poppies blazed in a grainfield goldening toward harvest. On the right stretched the manifold greens of a pasture where cattle drowsed beneath a broad-crowned oak. Man and woman rode side by side. Hoofs thumped softly, saddle leather creaked, the sweet smell of horse mingled with herbal pungencies, a blackbird whistled.

"No, I don't suppose Gaia will ever restart any program she's terminated," Laurinda said. "But it's no worse than death, and death is seldom that easy."

"The scale of it," Christian protested, then sighed. "But I daresay Wayfarer will tell me I'm being sloppy sentimental, and when I've rejoined him I'll agree." Wryness added that that had better be true. He would no longer be separate, an avatar, he would be one with a far greater entity, which would in its turn remerge with a greater one still.

"Without Gaia, they would never have existed, those countless lives, generation after generation after generation," Laurinda said. "Their worst miseries they brought on themselves. If any of them are ever to find their way to something better, truly better, she has to keep making fresh starts."

"M-m, I can't help remembering all the millennialists and utopians who slaughtered people wholesale, or tortured them or threw them into concentration camps, if their behavior didn't fit the convenient attainment of the inspired vision."

"No, no, it's not like that! Don't you see? She gives them their freedom to be themselves and, and to become more."

"Seems to me she adjusts the parameters and boundary conditions till the setup looks promising before she lets the experiment run." Christian frowned. "But I admit, it isn't believable that she does it simply because she's . . . bored and lonely. Not when the whole fellowship of her kind is open to her. Maybe we haven't the brains to know what her reasons are. Maybe she's explaining them to Wayfarer, or directly to Alpha," although communication among the stars would take decades at least.

"Do you want to go on nonetheless?" she asked.

"I said I do. I'm supposed to. But you?"

"Yes. I don't want to, well, fail her."

"I'm sort of at a loss what to try next, and not sure it's wise to let the amulets decide."

"But they can help us, counsel us." Laurinda drew breath. "Please. If you will. The next world we go to— could it be gentle? That horror we saw—"

He reached across to take her hand. "Exactly what I was thinking. Have you a suggestion?"

She nodded. "York Minster. It was in sad condition when I . . . lived . . . but I saw pictures and—It was one of the loveliest churches ever built, in the loveliest old town."

"Excellent idea. Not another lifeless piece of archive, though. A complete environment." Christian pondered. "We'll inquire first, naturally, but offhand I'd guess the Edwardian period would suit us well. On the Continent they called it the *belle époque*."

"Splendid!" she exclaimed. Already her spirits were rising anew.


# 7

Transfer.

They arrived near the west end, in the south aisle. Worshippers were few, scattered closer to the altar rail. In the dimness, under the glories of glass and soaring perpendicular arches, their advent went unobserved. Windows in that direction glowed more vividly—rose, gold, blue, the cool gray-green of the Five Sisters—than the splendor above their backs; it was a Tuesday morning in June. Incense wove its odor through the ringing chant from the choir.

Christian tautened. "That's Latin," he whispered. "In England, 1900?" He glanced down at his garments and hers, and peered ahead. Shirt, coat, trousers for him, with a hat laid on the pew; ruffled blouse, ankle-length gown, and lacy bonnet for her; but—"The clothes aren't right either."

"Hush," Laurinda answered as low. "Wait. We were told this wouldn't be our 1900. Here may be the only York Minster in all of Gaia."

He nodded stiffly. It was clear that the node had never attempted a perfect reproduction of any past milieu—impossible, and pointless to boot. Often, though not necessarily always, she took an approximation as a starting point; but it never went on to the same destiny. What were the roots of this day?

"Relax," Laurinda urged. "It's beautiful."

He did his best, and indeed the Roman Catholic mass at the tierce hour sang some tranquility into his heart.

After the Nunc Dimittis, when clergy and laity had departed, the two could wander around and savor. Emerging at last, they spent a while looking upon the carven tawny limestone of the front. This was no Parthenon; it was a different upsurging of the same miracle. But around it lay a world to discover. With half a sigh and half a smile, they set forth.

The delightful narrow "gates," walled in with half-timbered houses, lured them. More modern streets and buildings, above all the people therein, captured them. York was a living town, a market town, core of a wide hinterland, node of a nation. It racketed, it bustled.

The half smile faded. A wholly foreign setting would not have felt as wrong as one that was half-homelike.

Clothing styles were not radically unlike what pictures and historical dramas had once shown; but they were not identical. The English chatter was in no dialect of English known to Christian or Laurinda, and repeatedly they heard versions of German. A small, high-stacked steam locomotive pulled a train into a station of somehow Teutonic architecture. No early automobiles stuttered along the thoroughfares. Horse-drawn vehicles moved crowdedly, but the pavements were clean and the smell of dung faint because the animals wore a kind of diapers. A flag above a post office (?), fluttering in the wind, displayed a cross of St. Andrew on which was superimposed a two-headed gold eagle. A man with a megaphone bellowed at the throng to stand aside and make way for a military squadron. In blue uniforms, rifles on shoulders, they quick-marched to commands barked in German. Individual soldiers, presumably on leave, were everywhere. A boy went by, shrilly hawking newspapers, and Christian saw WAR in a headline.

"Listen, amulet," he muttered finally, "where can we get a beer?"

"A public house will admit you if you go in by the couples' entrance," replied the soundless voice.

So, no unescorted women allowed. Well, Christian thought vaguely, hadn't that been the case in his Edwardian years, at any rate in respectable taverns? A signboard jutting from a Tudor façade read GEORGE AND DRAGON. The wainscoted room inside felt equally English.

Custom was plentiful and noisy, tobacco smoke thick, but he and Laurinda found a table in a corner where they could talk without anybody else paying attention. The brew that a barmaid fetched was of Continental character. He didn't give it the heed it deserved.

"I don't think we've found our peaceful world after all," he said.

Laurinda looked beyond him, into distances where he

could not follow. "Will we ever?" she wondered. "Can any be, if it's human?"

He grimaced. "Well, let's find out what the hell's going on here."

"You can have a detailed explanation if you wish," said the voice in their heads. "You would be better advised to accept a bare outline, as you did before."

"Instead of loading ourselves down with the background of a world that never was," he mumbled.

"That never was ours," Laurinda corrected him.

"Carry on."

"This sequence was generated as of its fifteenth century C.E.," said the voice. "The conciliar movement was made to succeed, rather than failing as it did in your history."

"Uh, conciliar movement?"

"The ecclesiastical councils of Constance and later of Basel attempted to heal the Great Schism and reform the government of the Church. Here they accomplished it, giving back to the bishops some of the power that over the centuries had accrued to the popes, working out a reconciliation with the Hussites, and making other important changes. As a result, no Protestant breakaway occurred, nor wars of religion, and the Church remained a counterbalance to the state, preventing the rise of absolute monarchies."

"Why, that's wonderful," Laurinda whispered.

"Not too wonderful by now," Christian said grimly. "What happened?"

"In brief, Germany was spared the devastation of the Thirty Years' War and a long-lasting division into quarrelsome principalities. It was unified in the seventeenth century and soon became the dominant European power, colonizing and conquering eastward. Religious and cultural differences from the Slavs proved irreconcilable. As the harsh imperium provoked increasing restlessness, it perforce grew more severe, causing more rebellion. Meanwhile it decayed within, until today it has broken apart and the Russians are advancing on Berlin."

"I see. What about science and technology?"

"They have developed more slowly than in your history, although you have noted the existence of a fossil-fueled industry and inferred an approximately Lagrangian level of theory."

"The really brilliant eras were when all hell broke loose, weren't they?" Christian mused. "This Europe went through less agony, and invented and discovered less. Coincidence?"

"What about government?" Laurinda asked.

"For a time, parliaments flourished, more powerful than kings, emperors, or popes," said the voice. "In most Western countries they still wield considerable influence."

"As the creatures of special interests, I'll bet," Christian rasped. "All right, what comes next?"

Gaia knew. He sat in a reactivation of something she probably played to a finish thousands of years ago.

"Scientific and technological advance proceeds, accelerating, through a long period of general turbulence. At the termination point—"

"Never mind!" Oblivion might be better than a nuclear war.

Silence fell at the table. The life that filled the pub with its noise felt remote, unreal.

"We dare not weep," Laurinda finally said. "Not yet."

Christian shook himself. "Europe was never the whole of Earth," he growled. "How many worlds has Gaia made?"

"Many," the voice told him.

"Show us one that's really foreign. If you agree, Laurinda."

She squared her shoulders. "Yes, do." After a moment: "Not here. If we disappeared it would shock them. It might change the whole future."

"Hardly enough to notice," Christian said. "And would it matter in the long run? But, yeh, let's be off."

They wandered out, among marvels gone meaningless, until they found steps leading up onto the medieval wall. Thence they looked across roofs and river and Yorkshire beyond, finding they were alone.

"Now take us away," Christian ordered.

"You have not specified any type of world," said the voice.

"Surprise us."


# 8


Transfer.

The sky stood enormous, bleached blue, breezes warm underneath. A bluff overlooked a wide brown river. Trees grew close to its edge, tall, pale of bark, leaves silver-green and shivery. Christian recognized them, cottonwoods. He was somewhere in west central North America, then. Uneasy shadows lent camouflage if he and Laurinda kept still. Across the river the land reached broad, roads twisting their way through cultivation—mainly wheat and Indian corn—that seemed to be parceled out among small farms, each with its buildings, house, barn, occasional stable or workshop. The sweeping lines of the ruddy-tiled roofs looked Asian. He spied oxcarts and a few horseback riders on the roads, workers in the fields, but at their distance he couldn't identify race or garb. Above yonder horizon thrust clustered towers that also suggested the Orient. If they belonged to a city, it must be compact, not sprawling over the countryside but neatly drawn into itself.

One road ran along the farther riverbank. A procession went upon it. An elephant led, as richly caparisoned as the man under the silk awning of a howdah. Shaven-headed men in yellow robes walked after, flanked by horsemen who bore poles from which pennons streamed scarlet and gold. The sound of slowly beaten gongs and minor-key chanting came faint through the wind.

Christian snapped his fingers. "Stupid me!" he muttered. "Give us a couple of opticals."

Immediately he and Laurinda held the devices. From his era, they fitted into the palm but projected an image at any magnification desired, with no lenses off which light could glint to betray. He peered back and forth for minutes. Yes, the appearance was quite Chinese, or Chinese-derived, except that a number of the individuals he studied had more of an Amerindian countenance and the leader on the elephant wore a feather bonnet above his robe.

"How quiet here," Laurinda said.

"You are at the height of the Great Tranquility" the amulet voice answered.

"How many like that were there ever?" Christian wondered. "Where, when, how?"

"You are in North America, in the twenty-second century by your reckoning. Chinese navigators arrived on the Pacific shore seven hundred years ago, and colonists followed."

*In this world*, Christian thought, *Europe and Africa are surely a sketch, mere geography, holding a few primitive tribes at most, unless nothing is there but ocean. Simplify, simplify.*

"Given the distances to sail and the dangers, the process was slow," the voice went on. "While the newcomers displaced or subjugated the natives wherever they settled, most remained free for a long time, acquired the technology, and also developed resistance to introduced diseases. Eventually, being on roughly equal terms, the races began to mingle, genetically and culturally. The settlers mitigated the savagery of the religions they had encountered, but learned from the societies, as well as teaching. You behold the outcome."

"The Way of the Buddha?" Laurinda asked very softly.

"As influenced by Taoism and local nature cults. It is a harmonious faith, without sects or heresies, pervading the civilization."

"Everything can't be pure loving kindness," Christian said.

"Certainly not. But the peace that the Emperor Wei Zhi-fu brought about has lasted for a century and will for another two. If you travel, you will find superb achievements in the arts and in graciousness."

"Another couple of centuries." Laurinda's tone wavered the least bit. "Afterward?"

"It doesn't last," Christian predicted. "These are humans too. And—tell me—do they ever get to a real science?"

"No," said the presence. "Their genius lies in other realms. But the era of warfare to come will drive the development of a remarkable empirical technology."

"What era?"

"China never recognized the independence that this country proclaimed for itself, nor approved of its miscegenation. A militant dynasty will arise, which overruns a western hemisphere weakened by the religious and secular quarrels that do at last break out."

"And the conquerors will fall in their turn. Unless Gaia makes an end first. She does—she did—sometime, didn't she?"

"All things are finite. Her creations too."

The leaves rustled through muteness.

"Do you wish to go into the city and look about?" asked the presence. "It can be arranged for you to meet some famous persons."

"No," Christian said. "Not yet, anyway. Maybe later."

Laurinda sighed. "We'd rather go home now and rest."

"And think," Christian said. "Yes."

# 9

Transfer.

The sun over England seemed milder than for America. Westering, it sent rays through windows to glow in wood, caress marble and the leather bindings of books, explode into rainbows where they met cut glass, evoke flower aromas from a jar of potpourri.

Laurinda opened a bureau drawer. She slipped the chain of her amulet over her head and tossed the disc in. Christian blinked, nodded, and followed suit. She closed the drawer.

"We do need to be by ourselves for a while," she said. "This hasn't been a dreadful day like, like before, but I am so tired."

"Understandable," he replied.

"You?"

"I will be soon, no doubt."

"Those worlds—already they feel like dreams I've wakened from."

"An emotional retreat from them, I suppose. Not cowardice, no, no, just a necessary, temporary rest. You shared their pain. You're too sweet for your own good, Laurinda."

She smiled. "How you misjudge me. I'm not quite ready to collapse yet, if you aren't."

"Thunder, no."

She took crystal glasses out of a cabinet, poured from a decanter on a sideboard, and gestured invitation. The port fondled their tongues. They stayed on their feet, look meeting look.

"I daresay we'd be presumptuous and foolish to try finding any pattern, this early in our search," she ventured. "Those peeks we've had, out of who knows how many worlds—each as real as we are." She shivered.

"I may have a hunch," he said slowly.

"A what?"

"An intimation, an impression, a wordless kind of guess. Why has Gaia been doing it? I can't believe it's nothing but pastime."

"Nor I. Nor can I believe she would let such terrible things happen if she could prevent them. How can an intellect, a soul, like hers be anything but good?"

So Laurinda thought, Christian reflected; but she was an avatar of Gaia. He didn't suppose that affected the fairness of her conscious mind; he had come to know her rather well. But neither did it prove the nature, the ultimate intent, of Earth's node. It merely showed that the living Laurinda Ashcroft had been a decent person.

She took a deep draught from her glass before going on: "I think, myself, she is in the same position as the traditional God. Being good, she wants to share existence with others, and so creates them. But to make them puppets, automatons, would be senseless. They have to have consciousness and free will. Therefore they are able to sin, and do, all too often."

"Why hasn't she made them morally stronger?"

"Because she's chosen to make them human. And what are we but a specialized African ape?" Laurinda's tone lowered; she stared into the wine. "Specialized to make tools and languages and dreams; but the dreams can be nightmares."

In Gaia's and Alpha's kind laired no ancient beast, Christian thought. The human elements in them were long since absorbed, tamed, transfigured. His resurrection and hers must be nearly unique.

Not wanting to hurt her, he shaped his phrases with care. "Your idea is reasonable, but I'm afraid it leaves some questions dangling. Gaia does intervene, again and again. The amulets admit it. When the emulations get too far off track, she changes them and their people." Until she shuts them down, he did not add. "Why is she doing it, running history after history, experiment after experiment—why?"

Laurinda winced. "To, to learn about this strange race of ours?"

He nodded. "Yes, that's my hunch. Not even she, nor the galactic brain itself, can take first principles and compute what any human situation will lead to. Human affairs are chaotic. But chaotic systems do have structures, attractors, constraints. By letting things happen, through countless variations, you might discover a few general laws, which courses are better and which worse." He tilted his goblet. "To what end, though? There are no more humans in the outside universe. There haven't been for—how many million years? No, unless it actually is callous curiosity, I can't yet guess what she's after."

"Nor I." Laurinda finished her drink. "Now I am growing very tired, very fast."

"I'm getting that way too." Christian paused. "How about we go sleep till evening? Then a special dinner, and our heads ought to be more clear."

Briefly, she took his hand. "Until evening, dear friend."

# 10

The night was young and gentle. A full moon dappled the garden. Wine had raised a happy mood, barely tinged with wistfulness. Gravel scrunched rhythmically underfoot as Laurinda and Christian danced, humming the waltz melody together. When they were done, they sat down, laughing, by the basin. Brightness from above overflowed it. He had earlier put his amulet back on just long enough to command that a guitar appear for him. Now he took it up. He had never seen anything more beautiful than she was in the moonlight. He sang a song to her that he had made long ago when he was mortal.

"Lightfoot, Lightfoot, lead the measure
As we dance the summer in!
'Lifetime is our only treasure.
Spend it well, on love and pleasure,'
Warns the lilting violin.

"If we'll see the year turn vernal
Once again, lies all with chance.
Yes, this ordering's infernal,
But we'll make our own eternal
Fleeting moment where we dance.

"So shall we refuse compliance
When across the green we whirl,
Giving entropy defiance,

*Strings and winds in our alliance.*
*Be a victor. Kiss me, girl!"*

Suddenly she was in his arms.

## ∞ VIII ∞

Where the hills loomed highest above the river that cut through them, a slope on the left bank rose steep but thinly forested. Kalava directed the lifeboat carrying his party to land. The slaves at the oars grunted with double effort. Sweat sheened on their skins and runneled down the straining bands of muscle; it was a day when the sun blazed from a sky just half clouded. The prow grated on a sandbar in the shallows. Kalava told off two of his sailors to stand guard over boat and rowers. With the other four and Ilyandi, he waded ashore and began to climb.

It went slowly but stiffly. On top they found a crest with a view that snatched a gasp from the woman and a couple of amazed oaths from the men. Northward the terrain fell still more sharply, so that they looked over treetops down to the bottom of the range and across a valley awash with the greens and russets of growth. The river shone through it like a drawn blade, descending from dimly seen foothills and the sawtooth mountains beyond them. Two swordwings hovered on high, watchful for prey. Sunbeams shot past gigantic cloudbanks, filling their whiteness with cavernous shadows. Somehow the air felt cooler here, and the herbal smells gave benediction.

"It is fair, ai, it is as fair as the Sunset Kingdom of legend," Ilyandi breathed at last.

She stood slim in the man's kirtle and buskins that she, as a Vilku, could with propriety wear on trek. The wind fluttered her short locks. The coppery skin was as wet and almost as odorous as Kalava's midnight black, but she was no more wearied than any of her companions.

The sailor Urko scowled at the trees and underbrush crowding close on either side. Only the strip up which the travelers had come was partly clear, perhaps because of a landslide in the past. "Too much woods," he grumbled. It had, in fact, been a struggle to move about wherever they landed. They could not attempt the hunting that had been easy on the coast. Luckily, the water teemed with fish.

"Logging will cure that." Kalava's words throbbed. "And then what farms!" He stared raptly into the future.

Turning down-to-earth: "But we've gone far enough, now that we've gained an idea of the whole country. Three days, and I'd guess two more going back downstream. Any longer, and the crew at the ship could grow fearful. We'll turn around here."

"Other ships will bring other explorers," Ilyandi said.

"Indeed they will. And I'll skipper the first of them."

A rustling and crackling broke from the tangle to the right, through the boom of the wind. "What's that?" barked Taltara.

"Some big animal," Kalava replied. "Stand alert."

The mariners formed a line. Three grounded the spears they carried, the fourth unslung a crossbow from his shoulders and armed it. Kalava waved Ilyandi to go behind them and drew his sword.

The thing parted a brake and trod forth into the open.

"Aah!" wailed Yarvonin. He dropped his spear and whirled about to flee.

"Stand fast!" Kalava shouted. "Urko, shoot whoever runs, if I don't cut him down myself. Hold, you whoresons, hold!"

The thing stopped. For a span of many hammering heartbeats, none moved.

It was a sight to terrify. Taller by a head than the tallest man it sheered, but that head was faceless save for a horrible blank mask. Two thick arms sprouted from either side, the lower pair of hands wholly misshapen. A humped back did not belie the sense of their strength. As the travelers watched, the thing sprouted a skeletal third leg, to stand better on the uneven ground. Whether it was naked or armored in plate, in this full daylight it bore the hue of dusk.

"Steady, boys, steady," Kalava urged between clenched teeth. Ilyandi stepped from shelter to join him. An eldritch calm was upon her. "My lady, what *is* it?" he appealed.

"A god, or a messenger from the gods, I think." He could barely make her out beneath the wind.

"A demon," Eivala groaned, though he kept his post.

"No, belike not. We Vilkui have some knowledge of these matters. But, true, it is not fiery—and I never thought I would meet one—in this life—"

Ilyandi drew a long breath, briefly knotted her fists, then moved to take stance in front of the men. Having touched the withered sprig of tekin pinned at her breast, she covered her eyes and genuflected before straightening again to confront the mask.

The thing did not move, but, mouthless, it spoke, in a deep and resonant voice. The sounds were incomprehensible. After a moment it ceased, then spoke anew in an equally alien tongue. On its third try, Kalava exclaimed, "Hoy, that's from the Shining Fields!"

The thing fell silent, as if considering what it had heard. Thereupon words rolled out in the Ulonaian of Sirsu. "Be not afraid. I mean you no harm."

"What a man knows is little, what he understands is less, therefore let him bow down to wisdom," Ilyandi recited. She turned her head long enough to tell her companions: "Lay aside your weapons. Do reverence."

Clumsily, they obeyed.

In the blank panel of the blank skull appeared a man's visage. Though it was black, the features were not quite like anything anyone had seen before, nose broad, lips heavy, eyes round, hair tightly curled. Nevertheless, to spirits half stunned the magic was vaguely reassuring.

Her tone muted but level, Ilyandi asked, "What would you of us, lord?"

"It is hard to say," the strange one answered. After a pause: "Bewilderment goes through the world. I too. . . . You may call me Brannock."

The captain rallied his courage. "And I am Kalava, Kurvo's son, of Clan Samayoki." Aside to Ilyandi, low: "No disrespect that I don't name you, my lady. Let him work any spells on me." Despite the absence of visible genitals, already the humans thought of Brannock as male.

"My lord needs no names to work his will," she said. "I am hight Ilyandi, Lytin's daughter, born into Clan Arvala, now a Vilku of the fifth rank."

Kalava cleared his throat and added, "By your leave, lord, we'll not name the others just yet. They're scared aplenty as is." He heard a growl at his back and inwardly grinned. Shame would help hold them steady. As for him, dread was giving way to a thrumming keenness.

"You do not live here, do you?" Brannock asked.

"No," Kalava said, "we're scouts from overseas."

Ilyandi frowned at his presumption and addressed Brannock: "Lord, do we trespass? We knew not this ground was forbidden."

"It isn't," the other said. "Not exactly. But—" The face in the panel smiled. "Come, ease off, let us talk. We've much to talk about."

"He sounds not unlike a man," Kalava murmured to Ilyandi.

She regarded him. "If you be the man."

Brannock pointed to a big old gnarlwood with an overarching canopy of leaves. "Yonder is shade." He retracted his third leg and strode off. A fallen log took up most of the space. He leaned over and dragged it aside. Kalava's whole gang could not have done so. The action was not really necessary, but the display of power, benignly used, encouraged them further. Still, it was with hushed awe that the crewmen sat down in the paintwort. The captain, the Vilku, and the strange one remained standing.

"Tell me of yourselves," Brannock said mildly.

"Surely you know, lord," Ilyandi replied.

"That is as may be."

"He wants us to," Kalava said.

In the course of the next short while, prompted by questions, the pair gave a barebones account. Brannock's head within his head nodded. "I see. You are the first humans ever in this country. But your people have lived a long time in their homeland, have they not?"

"From time out of mind, lord," Ilyandi said, "though legend holds that our forebears came from the south."

Brannock smiled again. "You have been very brave to meet me like this, m-m-my lady. But you did tell your friend that your order has encountered beings akin to me?"

"You heard her whisper, across half a spearcast?" Kalava blurted.

"Or you hear us think, lord," Ilyandi said.

Brannock turned grave. "No. Not that. Else why would I have needed your story?"

"Dare I ask whence you come?"

"I shall not be angry. But it is nothing I can quite explain. You can help by telling me about those beings you know of."

Ilyandi could not hide a sudden tension. Kalava stiffened beside her. Even the dumbstruck sailors must have wondered whether a god would have spoken thus.

Ilyandi chose her words with care. "Beings from on high have appeared in the past to certain Vilkui or, sometimes, chieftains. They gave commands as to what the folk should or should not do. Ofttimes those commands were hard to fathom. Why must the Kivalui build watermills in the Swift River, when they had ample slaves to grind their grain?—But knowledge was imparted, too, counsel about where and how to search out the ways of nature. Always, the high one forbade open talk about his coming. The accounts lie in the secret annals of the Vilkui. But to you, lord—"

"What did those beings look like?" Brannock demanded sharply.

"Fiery shapes, winged or manlike, voices like great trumpets—"

"Ruvio's ax!" burst from Kalava. "The thing that passed overhead at sea!"

The men on the ground shuddered.

"Yes," Brannock said, most softly, "I may have had a part there. But as for the rest—"

His face flickered and vanished. After an appalling moment it reappeared.

"I am sorry, I meant not to frighten you, I forgot," he said. The expression went stony, the voice tolled. "Hear me. There is war in heaven. I am cast away from a battle, and enemy hunters may find me at any time. I carry a word that must, it is vital that it reach a certain place, a . . . a holy mountain in the north. Will you give aid?"

Kalava gripped his sword hilt so that it was as if the skin would split across his knuckles. The blood had left Ilyandi's countenance. She stood ready to be blasted with fire while she asked, "Lord Brannock, how do we know you are of the gods?"

Nothing struck her down. "I am not," he told her. "I too can die. But they whom I serve, they dwell in the stars."

The multitude of mystery, seen only when night clouds parted, but skythinkers taught that they circled always around the Axle of the North. . . . Ilyandi kept her back straight. "Then can you tell me of the stars?"

"You are intelligent as well as brave," Brannock said. "Listen."

Kalava could not follow what passed between those two. The sailors cowered.

At the end, with tears upon her cheekbones, Ilyandi stammered, "Yes, he knows the constellations, he knows of the ecliptic and the precession and the returns of the Great Comet, he is from the stars. Trust him. We, we dare not do otherwise."

Kalava let go his weapon, brought hand to breast in salute, and asked, "How can we poor creatures help you, lord?"

"*You* are the news I bear," said Brannock.

"What?"

"I have no time to explain—if I could. The hunters

may find me at any instant. But maybe, maybe you could go on for me after they do."

"Escaping what overpowered you?" Kalava's laugh rattled. "Well, a man might try."

"The gamble is desperate. Yet if we win, choose your reward, whatever it may be, and I think you shall have it."

Ilyandi lowered her head above folded hands. "Enough to have served those who dwell beyond the moon."

"Humph," Kalava could not keep from muttering, "if they want to pay for it, why not?" Aloud, almost eagerly, his own head raised into the wind that tossed his whitened mane: "What'd you have us do?"

Brannock's regard matched his. "I have thought about this. Can one of you come with me? I will carry him, faster than he can go. As for what happens later, we will speak of that along the way."

The humans stood silent.

"If I but had the woodcraft," Ilyandi then said. "Ai, but I would! To the stars!"

Kalava shook his head. "No, my lady. You go back with these fellows. Give heart to them at the ship. Make them finish the repairs." He glanced at Brannock. "How long will this foray take, lord?"

"I can reach the mountaintop in two days and a night," the other said. "If I am caught and you must go on alone, I think a good man could make the whole distance from here in ten or fifteen days."

Kalava laughed, more gladly than before. "*Courser* won't be seaworthy for quite a bit longer than that. Let's away." To Ilyandi: "If I'm not back by the time she's ready, sail home without me."

"No—" she faltered.

"Yes. Mourn me not. What a faring!" He paused. "May all be ever well with you, my lady."

"And with you, forever with you, Kalava," she answered, not quite steadily, "in this world and afterward, out to the stars."

From withes and vines torn loose and from strips taken off clothing or sliced from leather belts, Brannock fashioned a sort of carrier for his ally. The man assisted. However excited, he had taken on a matter-of-fact practicality. Brannock, who had also been a sailor, found it weirdly moving to see bowlines and sheet bends grow between deft fingers, amidst all this alienness.

Harnessed to his back, the webwork gave Kalava a seat and something to cling to. Radiation from the nuclear powerplant within Brannock was negligible; it employed quantum-tunneling fusion. He set forth, down the hills and across the valley.

His speed was not very much more than a human could have maintained for a while. If nothing else, the forest impeded him. He did not want to force his way through, leaving an obvious trail. Rather, he parted the brush before him or detoured around the thickest stands. His advantage lay in tirelessness. He could keep going without pause, without need for food, water, or sleep, as long as need be. The heights beyond might prove somewhat trickier. However, Mount Mindhome did not reach above timberline on this oven of an Earth, although growth became more sparse and dry with altitude. Roots should keep most slopes firm, and he would not encounter snow or ice.

Alien, yes. Brannock remembered cedar, spruce, a lake where caribou grazed turf strewn with salmonberries and the wind streamed fresh, driving white clouds over a sky utterly blue. Here every tree, bush, blossom, flitting insect was foreign; grass itself no longer grew, unless it was ancestral to the thick-lobed carpeting of glades; the winged creatures aloft were not birds, and what beast cries he heard were in no tongue known to him.

Wayfarer's avatar walked on. Darkness fell. After a while, rain roared on the roof of leaves overhead. Such drops as got through to strike him were big and warm. Attuned to both the magnetic field and the rotation of the planet, his directional sense held him on course while an inertial integrator clocked off the kilometers he left behind.

The more the better. Gaia's mobile sensors were bound to spy on the expedition from Ulonai, as new and potentially troublesome a factor as it represented. Covertly watching, listening with amplification, Brannock had learned of the party lately gone upstream and hurried to intercept it—less likely to be spotted soon. He supposed she would have kept continuous watch on the camp and that a tiny robot or two would have followed Kalava, had not Wayfarer been in rapport with her. Alpha's emissary might too readily become aware that her attention was on something near and urgent, and wonder what.

She could, though, let unseen agents go by from time to time and flash their observations to a peripheral part of her. It would be incredible luck if one of them did not, at some point, hear the crew talking about the apparition that had borne away their captain.

Then what? Somehow she must divert Wayfarer for a while, so that a sufficient fraction of her mind could

direct machines of sufficient capability to find Brannock
and deal with him. He doubted he could again fight free.
Because she dared not send out her most formidable
entities or give them direct orders, those that came
would have their weaknesses and fallibilities. But they
would be determined, ruthless, and on guard against the
powers he had revealed in the aircraft. It was clear that
she was resolved to keep hidden the fact that humans
lived once more on Earth.

Why, Brannock did not know, nor did he waste mental
energy trying to guess. This must be a business of high
importance; and the implications went immensely further, a secession from the galactic brain. His job was to
get the information to Wayfarer.

He *might* come near enough to call it in by radio. The
emissary was not tuned in at great sensitivity, and no
relay was set up for the short-range transmitter. Neither
requirement had been foreseen. If Brannock failed to
reach the summit, Kalava was his forlorn hope.

In which case—"Are you tired?" he asked. They had
exchanged few words thus far.

"Bone-weary and plank-stiff," the man admitted. And
croak-thirsty too, Brannock heard.

"That won't do. You have to be in condition to move
fast. Hold on a little more, and we'll rest." Maybe the
plural would give Kalava some comfort. Seldom could a
human have been as alone as he was.

Springs were abundant in this wet country. Brannock's chemosensors led him to the closest. By then the
rain had stopped. Kalava unharnessed, groped his way
in the dark, lay down to drink and drink. Meanwhile
Brannock, who saw quite clearly, tore off fronded
boughs to make a bed for him. Kalava flopped onto it
and almost immediately began to snore.

Brannock left him. A strong man could go several

days without eating before he weakened, but it wasn't necessary. Brannock collected fruits that ought to nourish. He tracked down and killed an animal the size of a pig, brought it back to camp, and used his tool-hands to butcher it.

An idea had come to him while he walked. After a search he found a tree with suitable bark. It reminded him all too keenly of birch, although it was red-brown and odorous. He took a sheet of it, returned, and spent a time inscribing it with a finger-blade.

Dawn seeped gray through gloom. Kalava woke, jumped up, saluted his companion, stretched like a panther and capered like a goat, limbering himself. "That did good," he said. "I thank my lord." His glance fell on the rations. "And did you provide food? You are a kindly god."

"Not either of those, I fear," Brannock told him. "Take what you want, and we will talk."

Kalava first got busy with camp chores. He seemed to have shed whatever religious dread he felt and now to look upon the other as a part of the world—certainly to be respected, but the respect was of the kind he would accord a powerful, enigmatic, high-ranking man. A hardy spirit, Brannock thought. Or perhaps his culture drew no line between the natural and the supernatural. To a primitive, everything was in some way magical, and so when magic manifested itself it could be accepted as simply another occurrence.

If Kalava actually was primitive. Brannock wondered about that.

It was encouraging to see how competently he went about his tasks, a woodsman as well as a seaman. Having gathered dry sticks and piled them in a pyramid, he set them alight. For this, he took from the pouch at his belt a little hardwood cylinder and piston, a packet of tinder, and a sulfur-tipped sliver. Driven down, the piston heated trapped air to ignite the powder; he dipped his match in, brought it up aflame, and used it to start his fire. Yes, an inventive people. And the woman Ilyandi had an excellent knowledge of naked-eye astronomy. Given the rarity of clear skies, that meant many lifetimes of patient observation, record-keeping, and logic, which must include mathematics comparable to Euclid's.

What else?

While Kalava toasted his meat and ate, Brannock made inquiries. He learned of warlike city-states, their hinterlands divided among clans; periodic folkmoots where the freemen passed laws, tried cases, and elected leaders; an international order of sacerdotes, teachers, healers, and philosophers; aggressively expansive, sometimes piratical commerce; barbarians, erupting out of the ever-growing deserts and wastelands; the grim militarism that the frontier states had evolved in response; an empirical but intensive biological technology, which had bred an amazing variety of specialized plants and animals, including slaves born to muscular strength, moronic wits, and canine obedience. . . .

Most of the description emerged as the pair were again traveling. Real conversation was impossible when Brannock wrestled with brush, forded a stream in spate, or struggled up a scree slope. Still, even then they managed an occasional question and answer. Besides, after he had crossed the valley and entered the foothills he found the terrain rugged but less often boggy, the trees and undergrowth thinning out, the air slightly cooling.

Just the same, Brannock would not have gotten as much as he did, in the short snatches he had, were he merely human. But he was immune to fatigue and breathlessness. He had an enormous data store to draw

on. It included his studies of history and anthropology
as a young mortal, and gave him techniques for constructing a logic tree and following its best branches—
for asking the right, most probably useful questions.
What emerged was a bare sketch of Kalava's world. It
was, though, clear and cogent.

It horrified him.

Say rather that his Christian Brannock aspect recoiled from the brutality of it. His Wayfarer aspect reflected that this was more or less how humans had
usually behaved, and that their final civilization would
not have been stable without its pervasive artificial intelligences. His journey continued.

He broke it to let Kalava rest and flex. From that hill
the view swept northward and upward to the mountains.
They rose precipitously ahead, gashed, cragged, and
sheer where they were not wooded, their tops lost in a
leaden sky. Brannock pointed to the nearest, thrust forward out of their wall like a bastion.

"We are bound yonder," he said. "On the height is
my lord, to whom I must get my news."

"Doesn't he see you here?" asked Kalava.

Brannock shook his generated image of a head. "No.
He might, but the enemy engages him. He does not yet
know she is the enemy. Think of her as a sorceress who
deceives him with clever talk, with songs and illusions,
while her agents go about in the world. My word will
show him what the truth is."

Would it? Could it, when truth and rightness seemed
as formless as the cloud cover?

"Will she be alert against you?"

"To some degree. How much, I cannot tell. If I can
come near, I can let out a silent cry that my lord will
hear and understand. But if her warriors catch me before then, you must go on, and that will be hard. You

may well fail and die. Have you the courage?"

Kalava grinned crookedly. "By now, I'd better, hadn't I?"

"If you succeed, your reward shall be boundless."

"I own, that's one wind in my sails. But also—" Kalava paused. "Also," he finished quietly, "the lady Ilyandi wishes this."

Brannock decided not to go into that. He lifted the rolled-up piece of bark he had carried in a lower hand. "The sight of you should break the spell, but here is a message for you to give."

As well as he was able, he went on to describe the route, the site, and the module that contained Wayfarer, taking care to distinguish it from everything else around. He was not sure whether the spectacle would confuse Kalava into helplessness, but at any rate the man seemed resolute. Nor was he sure how Kalava could cross half a kilometer of paving—if he could get that far—without Gaia immediately perceiving and destroying him. Maybe Wayfarer would notice first. Maybe, maybe.

He, Brannock, was using this human being as consciencelessly as ever Gaia might have used any; and he did not know what his purpose was. What possible threat to the fellowship of the stars could exist, demanding that this little brief life be offered up? Nevertheless he gave the letter to Kalava, who tucked it inside his tunic.

"I'm ready," said the man, and squirmed back into harness. They traveled on.


2


The hidden hot sun stood at midafternoon when Brannock's detectors reacted. He felt it as the least quivering hum, but instantly knew it for the electronic sign of something midge-size approaching afar. A mobile mini-sensor was on his trail.

It could not have the sensitivity of the instruments in him, he had not yet registered, but it would be here faster than he could run, would see him and go off to notify stronger machines. They could not be distant either. Once a clue to him had been obtained, they would have converged from across the continent, perhaps across the globe.

He slammed to a halt. He was in a ravine where a waterfall foamed down into a stream that tumbled off to join the Remnant. Huge, feathery bushes and trees with serrated bronzy leaves enclosed him. Insects droned from flower to purple flower. His chemosensors drank heavy perfumes.

"The enemy scouts have found me," he said. "Go."

Kalava scrambled free and down to the ground but hesitated, hand on sword. "Can I fight beside you?"

"No. Your service is to bear my word. Go. Straightaway. Cover your trail as best you can. And your gods be with you."

"Lord!"

Kalava vanished into the brush. Brannock stood alone.

The human fraction of him melted into the whole and he was entirely machine life, logical, emotionally detached, save for his duty to Wayfarer, Alpha, and consciousness throughout the universe. *This is not a bad place to defend*, he thought. He had the ravine wall to shield his back, rocks at its foot to throw, branches to break off for clubs and spears. He could give the pursuit a hard time before it took him prisoner. Of course, it might decide to kill him with an energy beam, but probably it wouldn't. Best from Gaia's viewpoint was to capture him and change his memories, so that he returned with a report of an uneventful cruise on which he saw nothing of significance.

He didn't think that first her agents could extract his real memories. That would take capabilities she had never anticipated needing. Just to make the device that had tried to take control of him earlier must have been an extraordinary effort, hastily carried out. Now she was still more limited in what she could do. An order to duplicate and employ the device was simple enough that it should escape Wayfarer's notice. The design and commissioning of an interrogator was something else—not to mention the difficulty of getting the information clandestinely to her.

Brannock dared not assume she was unaware he had taken Kalava with him. Most likely it was a report from an agent, finally getting around to checking on the lifeboat party, that apprised her of his survival and triggered the hunt for him. But the sailors would have been frightened, bewildered, their talk disjointed and nearly meaningless. Ilyandi, that bright and formidable woman, would have done her best to forbid them saying anything helpful. The impression ought to be that Brannock only meant to pump Kalava about his people, before releasing him to make his way back to them and himself proceeding on toward Mindhome.

In any event, it would not be easy to track the man down. He was no machine, he was an animal among countless animals, and the most cunning of all. The kind of saturation search that would soon find him was debarred. Gaia might keep a tiny portion of her forces searching and a tiny part of her attention poised against him, but she would not take him very seriously. Why should she?

Why should Brannock? Forlorn hope in truth.

He made his preparations. While he waited for the onslaught, his spirit ranged beyond the clouds, out among the stars and the millions of years that his greater self had known.

The room was warm. It smelled of lovemaking and the roses Laurinda had set in a vase. Evening light diffused through gauzy drapes to wash over a big four-poster bed.

She drew herself close against Christian where he lay propped on two pillows. Her arm went across his breast, his over her shoulders. "I don't want to leave this," she whispered.

"Nor I," he said into the tumbling sweetness of her hair. "How could I want to?"

"I mean—what we are—what we've become to one another."

"I understand."

She swallowed. "I'm sorry. I shouldn't have said that. Can you forget I did?"

"Why?"

"You know. I can't ask you to give up returning to your whole being. I *don't* ask you to."

He stared before him.

"I just don't want to leave this house, this bed yet," she said desolately. "After these past days and nights, not yet."

He turned his head again and looked down into gray eyes that blinked back tears. "Nor I," he answered. "But I'm afraid we must."

"Of course. Duty."

And Gaia and Wayfarer. If they didn't know already that their avatars had been slacking, surely she, at least, soon would, through the amulets and their link to her. No matter how closely engaged with the other vast mind, she would desire to know from time to time what was going on within herself.

Christian drew a breath. "Let me say the same that you did. I, this I that I am, damned well does not care to be anything else but your lover."

"Darling, darling."

"But," he said after the kiss.

"Go on," she said, lips barely away from his. "Don't be afraid of hurting me. You can't."

He sighed. "I sure can, and you can hurt me. May neither of us ever mean to. It's bound to happen, though."

She nodded. "Because we're human." Steadfastly: "Nevertheless, because of you, that's what I hope to stay."

"I don't see how we can. Which is what my 'but' was about." He was quiet for another short span. "After we've remerged, after we're back in our onenesses, no doubt we'll feel differently."

"I wonder if I ever will, quite."

He did not remind her that this "I" of her would no longer exist save as a minor memory and a faint overtone. Instead, trying to console, however awkwardly, he said, "I think I want it for you, in spite of everything. Immortality. Never to grow old and die. The power, the awareness."

"Yes, I know. In these lives we're blind and deaf and stupefied." Her laugh was a sad little murmur. "I like it."

"Me too. We being what we are." Roughly: "Well, we have a while left to us."

"But we must get on with our task."

"Thank you for saying it for me."

"I think you realize it more clearly than I do. That makes it harder for you to speak." She lifted her hand to cradle his cheek. "We can wait till tomorrow, can't we?" she pleaded. "Only for a good night's sleep."

He made a smile. "Hm. Sleep isn't all I have in mind."

"We'll have other chances . . . along the way. Won't we?"


# 2

Early morning in the garden, flashes of dew on leaves and petals, a hawk aloft on a breeze that caused Laurinda to pull her shawl about her. She sat by the basin and looked up at him where he strode back and forth before her, hands clenched at his sides or clutched together at his back. Gravel grated beneath his feet.

"But where should we go?" she wondered. "Aimlessly drifting from one half-world to another till—they—finish their business and recall us. It seems futile." She attempted lightness. "I confess to thinking we may as well ask to visit the enjoyable ones."

He shook his head. "I'm sorry. I've been thinking differently." Even during the times that were theirs alone.

She braced herself.

"You know how it goes," he said. "Wrestling with ideas, and they have no shapes, then suddenly you wake and they're halfway clear. I did today. Tell me how it strikes you. After all, you represent Gaia."

He saw her wince. When he stopped and bent down to make a gesture of contrition, she told him quickly, "No, it's all right, dearest. Do go on."

He must force himself, but his voice gathered momentum as he paced and talked. "What have we seen to date? This eighteenth-century world, where Newton's not long dead, Lagrange and Franklin are active, Lavoisier's a boy, and the Industrial Revolution is getting under way. Why did Gaia give it to us for our home base? Just because here's a charming house and countryside? Or because this was the best choice for her out of all she has emulated?"

Laurinda had won back to calm. She nodded. "M-m, yes, she wouldn't create one simply for us, especially when she is occupied with Wayfarer."

"Then we visited a world that went through a similar stage back in its Hellenistic era," Christian went on. Laurinda shivered. "Yes, it failed, but the point is, we discovered it's the only Graeco-Roman history Gaia found worth continuing for centuries. Then the, uh, conciliar Europe of 1900. That was scientific-industrial too, maybe more successfully—or less unsuccessfully—on account of having kept a strong, unified Church, though it was coming apart at last. Then the Chinese-American—not scientific, very religious, but destined to produce considerable technology in its own time of troubles." He was silent a minute or two, except for his footfalls. "Four out of many, three almost randomly picked. Doesn't that suggest that all which interest her have something in common?"

"Why, yes," she said. "We've talked about it, you remember. It seems as if Gaia has been trying to bring her people to a civilization that is rich, culturally and spiritually as well as materially, and is kindly and will endure."

"Why," he demanded, "when the human species is extinct?"

She straightened where she sat. "It isn't! It lives again here, in her."

He bit his lip. "Is that the Gaia in you speaking, or the you in Gaia?"

"What do you mean?" she exclaimed.

He halted to stroke her head. "Nothing against you. Never. You are honest and gentle and everything else that is good." Starkly: "I'm not so sure about her."

"Oh, no." He heard the pain. "Christian, no."

"Well, never mind that for now," he said fast, and resumed his gait to and fro. "My point is this. Is it merely an accident that all four live worlds we've been in were oriented toward machine technology, and three of them toward science? Does Gaia want to find out what drives the evolution of societies like that?"

Laurinda seized the opening. "Why not? Science opens the mind, technology frees the body from all sorts of horrors. Here, today, Jenner and his smallpox vaccine aren't far in the future—"

"I wonder how much more there is to her intention. But anyway, my proposal is that we touch on the highest-tech civilization she has."

A kind of gladness kindled in her. "Yes, yes! It must be strange and wonderful."

He frowned. "For some countries, long ago in real history, it got pretty dreadful."

"Gaia wouldn't let that happen."

He abstained from reminding her of what Gaia did let happen, before changing or terminating it.

She sprang to her feet. "Come!" Seizing his hand, mischievously: "If we stay any length of time, let's arrange for private quarters."

# 3

In a room closed off, curtains drawn, Christian held an amulet in his palm and stared down at it as if it bore a face. Laurinda stood aside, listening, while her own countenance tightened with distress.

"It is inadvisable," declared the soundless voice.

"Why?" snapped Christian.

"You would find the environment unpleasant and the people incomprehensible."

"Why should a scientific culture be that alien to us?" asked Laurinda.

"And regardless," said Christian, "I want to see for myself. Now."

"Reconsider," urged the voice. "First hear an account of the milieu."

"No, *now*. To a safe locale, yes, but one where we can get a fair impression, as we did before. Afterward you can explain as much as you like."

"Why shouldn't we first hear?" Laurinda suggested.

"Because I doubt Gaia wants us to see," Christian answered bluntly. He might as well. Whenever Gaia chose, she could scan his thoughts. To the amulet, as if it were a person: "Take us there immediately, or Wayfarer will hear from me."

His suspicions, vague but growing, warned against giving the thing time to inform Gaia and giving her time to work up a Potemkin village or some other diversion. At the moment she must be unaware of this scene, her mind preoccupied with Wayfarer's, but she had probably made provision for being informed in a low-level—subconscious?—fashion at intervals, and anything alarming would catch her attention. It was also

likely that she had given the amulets certain orders beforehand, and now it appeared that among them was to
avoid letting him know what went on in that particular
emulation.

Why, he could not guess.

"You are being willful," said the voice.

Christian grinned. "And stubborn, and whatever else
you care to call it. Take us!"

Pretty clearly, he thought, the program was not capable of falsehoods. Gaia had not foreseen a need for
that; Christian was no creation of hers, totally known
to her, he was Wayfarer's. Besides, if Wayfarer noticed
that his avatar's guide could be a liar, that would have
been grounds for suspicion.

Laurinda touched her man's arm. "Darling, should
we?" she said unevenly. "She *is* the . . . the mother of all
this."

"A broad spectrum of more informative experiences
is available," argued the voice. "After them, you would
be better prepared for the visit you propose."

"Prepared," Christian muttered. That could be inter-
preted two ways. He and Laurinda might be conducted
to seductively delightful places while Gaia learned of
the situation and took preventive measures, meantime
keeping Wayfarer distracted. "I still want to begin with
your highest tech." To the woman: "I have my reasons.
I'll tell you later. Right now we have to hurry."

Before Gaia could know and act.

She squared her shoulders, took his free hand, and
said, "Then I am with you. Always."

"Let's go," Christian told the amulet.

# 4

Transfer.

The first thing he noticed, transiently, vividly, was that he and Laurinda were no longer dressed for eighteenth-century England, but in lightweight white blouses, trousers, and sandals. Headcloths flowed down over their necks. Heat smote. The air in his nostrils was parched, full of metallic odors. Half-heard rhythms of machinery pulsed through it and through the red-brown sand underfoot.

He tautened his stance and gazed around. The sky was overcast, a uniform gray in which the sun showed no more than a pallor that cast no real shadows. At his back the land rolled away ruddy. Man-high stalks with narrow bluish leaves grew out of it, evenly spaced about a meter apart. To his right, a canal slashed across, beneath a transparent deck. Ahead of him the ground was covered by different plants, if that was what they were, spongy, lobate, pale golden in hue. A few—creatures— moved around, apparently tending them, bipedal but shaggy and with arms that seemed trifurcate. A gigantic building or complex of buildings reared over that horizon, multiply tiered, dull white, though agleam with hundreds of panels that might be windows or might be something else. As he watched, an aircraft passed overhead. He could just see that it had wings and hear the drone of an engine.

Laurinda had not let go of his hand. She gripped hard. "This is no country I ever heard of," she said thinly.

"Nor I," he answered. "But I think I recognize—" To the amulets: "This isn't any re-creation of Earth in the past, is it? It's Earth today."

"Of approximately the present year," the voice admitted.

"We're not in Arctica, though."

"No. Well south, a continental interior. You required to see the most advanced technology in the emulations. Here it is in action."

Holding the desert at bay, staving off the death that ate away at the planet. Christian nodded. He felt confirmed in his idea that the program was unable to give him any outright lie. That didn't mean it would give him forthright responses.

"This is their greatest engineering?" Laurinda marveled. "We did—better—in my time. Or yours, Christian."

"They're working on it here, I suppose," the man said. "We'll investigate further. After all, this is a bare glimpse."

"You must remember," the voice volunteered, "no emulation can be as full and complex as the material universe."

"M-m, yeh. Skeletal geography, apart from chosen regions; parochial biology; simplified cosmos."

Laurinda glanced at featureless heaven. "The stars unreachable, because here they are not stars?" She shuddered and pressed close against him.

"Yes, a paradox," he said. "Let's talk with a scientist."

"That will be difficult," the voice demurred.

"You told us in Chinese America you could arrange meetings. It shouldn't be any harder in this place."

The voice did not reply at once. Unseen machines rumbled. A dust devil whirled up on a sudden gust of wind. Finally: "Very well. It shall be one who will not be stricken dumb by astonishment and fear. Nevertheless, I should supply you beforehand with a brief description of what you will come to."

"Go ahead. If it is brief."

What changes in the history would that encounter bring about? Did it matter? This world was evidently not in temporary reactivation, it was ongoing; the newcomers were at the leading edge of its timeline. Gaia could erase their visit from it. If she cared to. Maybe she was going to terminate it soon because it was making no further progress that interested her.

# 5

Transfer.

Remote in a wasteland, only a road and an airstrip joining it to anything else, a tower lifted from a walled compound. Around it, night was cooling in a silence hardly touched by a susurrus of chant where robed figures bearing dim lights did homage to the stars. Many were visible, keen and crowded amidst their darkness, a rare sight, for clouds had parted across most of the sky. More lights glowed muted on a parapet surrounding the flat roof of a tower. There a single man and his helper used the chance to turn instruments aloft, telescope, spectroscope, cameras, bulks in the gloom.

Christian and Laurinda appeared unto them.

The man gasped, recoiled for an instant, and dropped to his knees. His assistant caught a book that he had nearly knocked off a table, replaced it, stepped back, and stood imperturbable, an anthropoid whose distant ancestors had been human but who lived purely to serve his master.

Christian peered at the man. As his eyes adapted, he saw garments like his, embroidered with insignia of rank and kindred, headdress left off after dark. The skin was ebony black but nose and lips were thin, eyes oblique, fingertips tapered, long hair and closely trimmed beard straight and blond. *No race that ever inhabited old Earth,* Christian thought; *no, this is a breed that Gaia designed for the dying planet.*

The man signed himself, looked into the pale faces of the strangers, and said, uncertainly at first, then with a gathering strength: "Hail and obedience, messengers of God. Joy at your advent."

Christian and Laurinda understood, as they had understood hunted Zoe. The amulets had told them they would not be the first apparition these people had known. "Rise," Christian said. "Be not afraid."

"Nor call out," Laurinda added.

*Smart lass,* Christian thought. The ceremony down in the courtyard continued. "Name yourself," he directed.

The man got back on his feet and took an attitude deferential rather than servile. "Surely the mighty ones know," he said. "I am Eighth Khaltan, chief astrologue of the Ilgai Technome, and, and wholly unworthy of this honor." He hesitated. "Is that, dare I ask, is that why you have chosen the forms you show me?"

"No one has had a vision for several generations," explained the soundless voice in the heads of the newcomers.

"Gaia has manifested herself in the past?" Christian subvocalized.

"Yes, to indicate desirable courses of action. Normally the sending has had the shape of a fire."

"How scientific is *that?*"

Laurinda addressed Khaltan: "We are not divine messengers. We have come from a world beyond your world, as mortal as you, not to teach but to learn."

The man smote his hands together. "Yet it is a miracle, again a miracle—in my lifetime!"

Nonetheless he was soon avidly talking. Christian recalled myths of men who were the lovers of goddesses or who tramped the roads and sat at humble meat with God Incarnate. The believer accepts as the unbeliever cannot.

Those were strange hours that followed. Khaltan was not simply devout. To him the supernatural was another set of facts, another facet of reality. Since it lay beyond his ken, he had turned his attention to the measurable world. In it he observed and theorized like a Newton. Tonight his imagination blazed, questions exploded from him, but always he chose his words with care and turned everything he heard around and around in his mind, examining it as he would have examined some jewel fallen from the sky.

Slowly, piecemeal, while the stars wheeled around the pole, a picture of his civilization took shape. It had overrun and absorbed every other society—no huge accomplishment, when Earth was meagerly populated and most folk on the edge of starvation.

The major technology was biological, agronomy, aquaculture in the remnant lakes and seas, ruthlessly practical genetics. Industrial chemistry flourished. It joined with physics at the level of the later nineteenth century to enable substantial engineering works and reclamation projects.

Society itself—How do you summarize an entire culture in words? It can't be done. Christian got the impression of a nominal empire, actually a broad-based oligarchy of families descended from conquering soldiers. Much upward mobility was by adoption of promising commoners, whether children or adults. Sons who made no contribution to the well-being of the clan or who disgraced it could be kicked out, if somebody did not pick a fight and kill them in a duel. Unsatisfactory daughters were also expelled, unless a marriage into a lower class could be negotiated. Otherwise the status of the sexes was roughly equal; but this meant that women who chose to compete with men must do so on male terms. The nobles provided the commons with protection, courts of appeal, schools, leadership, and pageantry. In return they drew taxes, corvée, and general subordination; but in most respects the commoners were generally left to themselves. Theirs was not altogether a dog-eat-dog situation; they had institutions, rites, and hopes of their own. Yet many went to the wall, while the hard work of the rest drove the global economy.

*It's not a deliberately cruel civilization,* Christian thought, *but neither is it an especially compassionate one.*

Had any civilization ever been, really? Some fed their poor, but mainly they fed their politicians and bureaucrats.

He snatched his information out of talk that staggered everywhere else. The discourse for which Khaltan yearned was of the strangers' home—he got clumsily evasive, delaying responses—and the whole system of the universe, astronomy, physics, everything.

"We dream of rockets going to the planets. We have tried to shoot them to the moon," he said, and told of launchers that ought to have worked. "All failed."

*Of course,* Christian thought. Here the moon and planets, yes, the very sun were no more than lights. The tides rose and fell by decree. The Earth was a caricature of Earth outside. Gaia could do no better.

"Are we then at the end of science?" Khaltan cried once. "We have sought and sought for decades, and have won to nothing further than measurements more exact." Nothing that would lead to relativity, quantum theory, wave mechanics, their revolutionary insights and consequences. Gaia could not accommodate it. "The angels in the past showed us what to look for. Will you not? Nature holds more than we know. Your presence bears witness!"

"Later, perhaps later," Christian mumbled, and cursed himself for his falsity.

"Could we reach the planets—Caged, the warrior spirit turns inward on itself. Rebellion and massacre in the Westlands—"

Laurinda asked what songs the people sang.

Clouds closed up. The rite in the courtyard ended. Khaltan's slave stood motionless while he himself talked on and on.

The eastern horizon lightened. "We must go," Christian said.

"You will return?" Khaltan begged. "Ai-ha, you will?"

Laurinda embraced him for a moment. "Fare you well," she stammered, "fare always well."

How long would his "always" be?

# 6

After an uneasy night's sleep and a nearly wordless breakfast, there was no real cause to leave the house in England. The servants, scandalized behind carefully held faces, might perhaps eavesdrop, but would not comprehend, nor would any gossip that they spread make a difference. A deeper, unuttered need sent Christian and Laurinda forth. This could well be the last of their mornings.

They followed a lane to a hill about a kilometer away. Trees on its top did not obscure a wide view across the land. The sun stood dazzling in the east, a few small clouds sailed across a blue as radiant as their whiteness, but an early breath of autumn was in the wind. It went strong and fresh, scattering dawn-mists off plowland and sending waves through the green of pastures; it soughed in the branches overhead and whirled some already dying leaves off. High beyond them winged a V of wild geese.

For a while, man and woman stayed mute. Finally Laurinda breathed, savored, fragrances of soil and sky, and murmured, "That Gaia brought this back to life— She must be good. She loves the world."

Christian looked from her, aloft, and scowled before he made an oblique reply. "What are she and Wayfarer doing?"

"How can we tell?"—tell what the gods did or even where they fared. They were not three-dimensional beings, nor bound by the time that bound their creations.

"She's keeping him occupied," said Christian.

"Yes, of course. Taking him through the data, the whole of her stewardship of Earth."

"To convince him she's right in wanting to let the planet die."

"A tragedy—but in the end, everything is tragic, isn't it?" *Including you and me.* "What . . . we . . . they . . . can learn from the final evolution, that may well be worth it all, as the Acropolis was worth it all. The galactic brain itself can't foreknow what life will do, and life is rare among the stars."

Almost, he snapped at her. "I know, I know. How often have we been over this ground? How often have *they?* I might have believed it myself. But—"

Laurinda waited. The wind skirled, caught a stray lock of hair, tossed it about over her brow.

"But why has she put humans, not into the distant past"—Christian gestured at the landscape lying like an eighteenth-century painting around them—"but into now, an Earth where flesh-and-blood humans died eons ago?"

"She's in search of a fuller understanding, surely."

"Surely?"

Laurinda captured his gaze and held it. "I think she's been trying to find how humans can have, in her, the truly happy lives they never knew in the outer cosmos."

"Why should she care about that?"

"I don't know. I'm only human." Earnestly: "But could it be that that element in her is so strong—so many, many of us went into her—that she longs to see us happy, like a mother with her children?"

"All that manipulation, all those existences failed and discontinued. It doesn't seem very motherly to me."

"I don't know, I tell you!" she cried.

He yearned to comfort her, kiss away the tears caught in her lashes, but urgency drove him onward. "If the effort has no purpose except itself, it seems mad. Can a nodal mind go insane?"

She retreated from him, appalled. "No. Impossible."

"Are you certain? At least, the galactic brain has to know the truth, the whole truth, to judge whether something here has gone terribly wrong."

Laurinda forced a nod. "You will report to Wayfarer, and he will report to Alpha, and all the minds will decide," a question that was unanswerable by mortal creatures.

Christian stiffened. "I have to do it at once."

He had hinted, she had guessed, but just the same she seized both his sleeves and protest spilled wildly from her lips. "What? Why? No! You'd only disturb him in his rapport, and her. Wait till we're summoned. We have till then, darling."

"I want to wait," he said. Sweat stood on his skin,

though the blood had withdrawn. "God, I want to! But I don't dare."

"Why not?"

She let go of him. He stared past her and said fast, flattening the anguish out of his tones: "Look, she didn't want us to see that final world. She clearly didn't, or quite expect we'd insist, or she'd have been better prepared. Maybe she could have passed something else off on us. As is, once he learns, Wayfarer will probably demand to see for himself. And she does not want him particularly interested in her emulations. Else why hasn't she taken him through them directly, with me along to help interpret?

"Oh, I don't suppose our action has been catastrophic for her plans, whatever they are. She can still cope, can still persuade him these creations are merely . . . toys of hers, maybe. That is, she can if she gets the chance to. I don't believe she should."

"How can you take on yourself—How can you imagine—"

"The amulets are a link to her. Not a constantly open channel, obviously, but at intervals they must inform a fraction of her about us, and she must also be able to set up intervals when Wayfarer gets too preoccupied with what he's being shown to notice that a larger part of her attention has gone elsewhere. We don't know when that'll happen next. I'm going back to the house and tell her through one of the amulets that I require immediate contact with him."

Laurinda stared as if at a ghost.

"That will not be necessary," said the wind.

Christian lurched where he stood. "What?" he blurted. "You—"

"Oh—Mother—" Laurinda lifted her hands into emptiness.

The blowing of the wind, the rustling in the leaves made words. "The larger part of me, as you call it, has in fact been informed and is momentarily free. I was waiting for you to choose your course."

Laurinda half moved to kneel in the grass. She glanced at Christian, who had regained balance and stood with fists at sides, confronting the sky. She went to stand by him.

"My lady Gaia," Christian said most quietly, "you can do to us as you please," change or obliterate or whatever she liked, in a single instant; but presently Wayfarer would ask why. "I think you understand my doubts."

"I do," sighed the air. "They are groundless. My creation of the Technome world is no different from my creation of any other. My avatar said it for me: I give existence, and I search for ways that humans, of their free will, can make the existence good."

Christian shook his head. "No, my lady. With your intellect and your background, you must have known from the first what a dead end that world would soon be, scientists on a planet that is a sketch and everything else a shadow show. My limited brain realized it. No, my lady, as cold-bloodedly as you were experimenting, I believe you did all the rest in the same spirit. Why? To what end?"

"Your brain is indeed limited. At the proper time, Wayfarer shall receive your observations and your fantasies. Meanwhile, continue in your duty, which is to observe further and refrain from disturbing us in our own task."

"My duty is to report."

"In due course, I say." The wind-voice softened. "There are pleasant places besides this."

Paradises, maybe. Christian and Laurinda exchanged a glance that lingered for a second. Then she smiled the least bit, boundlessly sorrowfully, and shook her head.

"No," he declared, "I dare not."

He did not speak it, but he and she knew that Gaia knew what they foresaw. Given time, and they lost in their joy together, she could alter their memories too slowly and subtly for Wayfarer to sense what was happening.

Perhaps she could do it to Laurinda at this moment, in a flash. But she did not know Christian well enough. Down under his consciousness, pervading his being, was his aspect of Wayfarer and of her coequal Alpha. She would need to feel her way into him, explore and test with infinite delicacy, remake him detail by minutest detail, always ready to back off if it had an unexpected effect; and perhaps another part of her could secretly take control of the Technome world and erase the event itself. . . . She needed time, even she.

"Your action would be futile, you know," she said. "It would merely give me the trouble of explaining to him what you in your arrogance refuse to see."

"Probably. But I have to try."

The wind went bleak. "Do you defy me?"

"I do," Christian said. It wrenched from him: "Not my wish. It's Wayfarer in me. I, I cannot do otherwise. Call him to me."

The wind gentled. It went over Laurinda like a caress. "Child of mine, can you not persuade this fool?"

"No, Mother," the woman whispered. "He is what he is."

"And so—?"

Laurinda laid her hand in the man's. "And so I will go with him, forsaking you, Mother."

"You are casting yourselves from existence."

Christian's free fingers clawed the air. "No, not her!" he shouted. "She's innocent!"

"I am not," Laurinda said. She swung about to lay her arms around him and lift her face to his. "I love you."

"Be it as you have chosen," said the wind.

The dream that was the world fell into wreck and dissolved. Oneness swept over them like twin tides, each reclaiming a flung drop of spindrift; and the two seas rolled again apart.

The last few hundred man-lengths Kalava went mostly on his belly. From bush to bole he crawled, stopped, lay flat and strained every sense into the shadows around him, before he crept onward. Nothing stirred but the twigs above, buffeted on a chill and fitful breeze. Nothing sounded but their creak and click, the scrittling of such leaves as they bore, now and then the harsh cry of a hookbeak—those, and the endless low noise of demons, like a remote surf wherein shrilled flutes on no scale he knew, heard more through his skin than his ears but now, as he neared, into the blood and bone of him.

On this rough, steep height the forest grew sparse, though brush clustered thick enough, accursedly rustling as he pushed by. Everything was parched, branches brittle, most foliage sere and yellow-brown, the ground blanketed with tindery fallstuff. His mouth and gullet smoldered as dry. He had passed through fog until he saw from above that it was a layer of clouds spread to worldedge, the mountain peaks jutting out of it like teeth, and had left all rivulets behind him. Well before then, he had finished the meat Brannock provided, and had not lingered to hunt for more; but hunger was a small thing, readily forgotten when he drew nigh to death.

Over the dwarfish trees arched a deep azure. Sun-beams speared from the west, nearly level, to lose themselves in the woods. Whenever he crossed them, their touch burned. Never, not in the southern deserts or on the eastern Mummy Steppe, had he known a country this forbidding. He had done well to come so far, he thought. Let him die as befitted a man.

If only he had a witness, that his memory live on in song. Well, maybe Ilyandi could charm the story out of the gods.

Kalava felt no fear. He was not in that habit. What lay ahead engrossed him. How he would acquit himself concerned him.

Nonetheless, when finally he lay behind a log and peered over it, his head whirled and his heart stumbled.

Brannock had related truth, but its presence overwhelmed. Here at the top, the woods grew to the boundaries of a flat black field. Upon it stood the demons—or the gods—and their works. He saw the central, softly rainbowlike dome, towers like lances and towers like webwork, argent nets and ardent globes, the bulks and shapes everywhere around, the little flyers that flitted aglow, and more and more, all half veiled and ashimmer, aripple, apulse, while the life-beat of it went through him to make a bell of his skull, and it was too strange, his eyes did not know how to see it, he gaped as if blinded and shuddered as if pierced.

Long he lay powerless and defenseless. The sun sank down to the western clouds. Their deck went molten gold. The breeze strengthened. Somehow its cold reached to Kalava and wakened his spirit. He groped his way back toward resolution. Brannock had warned him it would be like this. Ilyandi had said Brannock was of the gods whom she served, her star-gods, hers. He had given his word to their messenger and to her.

He dug fingers into the soil beneath him. It was real, familiar, that from which he had sprung and to which he would return. Yes, he was a man.

He narrowed his gaze. Grown a bit accustomed, he saw that they yonder did, indeed, have shapes, however shifty, and places and paths. They were not as tall as the sky, they did not fling lightning bolts about or roar with thunder. Ai-ya, they were awesome, they were dreadful to behold, but they could do no worse than kill him. Could they? At least, he would try not to let them do worse. If they were about to capture him, his sword would be his friend, releasing him.

And . . . yonder, hard by the dome, yonder loomed the god of whom Brannock spoke, the god deceived by the sorceress. He bore the spearhead form, he sheened blue and coppery in the sunset light, when the stars came forth they would be a crown for him, even as Brannock foretold.

Had he been that which passed above the Windroad Sea? Kalava's heart thuttered.

How to reach him, across a hard-paved space amidst the many demons? After dark, creeping, a finger-length at a time, then maybe a final dash—

A buzz went by Kalava's temple. He looked around and saw a thing the size of a bug hovering. But it was metal, the light flashed off it, and was that a single eye staring at him?

He snarled and swatted. His palm smote hardness. The thing reeled in the air. Kalava scuttled downhill into the brush.

He had been seen. Soon the sorceress would know.

All at once he was altogether calm, save that his spirit thrummed like rigging in a gale. Traveling, he had thought what he might do if something like this proved to be in his doom. Now he would do it. He would divert the enemy's heed from himself, if only for a snatch of moments.

Quickly, steadily, he took the firemaker from his pouch, charged it, drove the piston in, pulled it out and inserted a match, brought up a little, yellow flame. He touched it to the withered bush before him. No need to puff. A leaf crackled instantly alight. The wind cast it against another, and shortly the whole shrub stood ablaze. Kalava was already elsewhere, setting more fires.

Keep on the move! The demon scouts could not be everywhere at a single time. Smoke began to sting his eyes and nostrils, but its haze swirled ever thicker, and the sun had gone under the clouds. The flames cast their own light, leaping, surging, as they climbed into the trees and made them torches.

Heat licked at Kalava. An ember fell to sear his left forearm. He barely felt it. He sped about on his work, himself a fire demon. Flyers darted overhead in the dusk. He gave them no heed either. Although he tried to make no noise except for the hurtful breaths he gasped, within him shouted a battle song.

When the fire stood like a wall along the whole southern edge of the field, when it roared like a beast or a sea, he ran from its fringe and out into the open.

Smoke was a bitter, concealing mist through which sparks rained. To and fro above flew the anxious lesser demons. Beyond them, the first stars were coming forth.

Kalava wove his way among the greater shapes. One stirred. It had spied him. Soundlessly, it flowed in pursuit. He dodged behind another, ran up and over the flanks of a low-slung third, sped on toward the opal dome and the god who stood beside it.

A thing with spines and a head like a cold sun slid in front of him. He tried to run past. It moved to block his

way, faster than he was. The first one approached. He
drew a blade and hoped it would bite on them before
he died.

From elsewhere came a being with four arms, two
legs, and a mask. "Brannock!" Kalava bawled. "Ai, Brannock, you got here!"

Brannock stopped, a spear-length away. He did not
seem to know the man. He only watched as the other
two closed in.

Kalava took stance. The old song rang in him:

*If the gods have left you,*
*Then laugh at them, warrior.*
*Never your heart*
*Will need to forsake you.*

He heard no more than the noise of burning. But
suddenly through the smoke he saw his foes freeze mov-
eless, while Brannock trod forward as boldly as ever before; and Kalava knew that the god of Brannock and
Ilyandi had become aware of him and had given a command.

Weariness torrented over him. His sword clattered to
the ground. He sank too, fumbled in his filthy tunic,
took out the message written on bark and offered it. "I
have brought you this," he mumbled. "Now let me go
back to my ship."

## ∞ XII ∞

We must end as we began, making a myth, if we would tell of that which we cannot ever really know. Imagine two minds conversing. The fire on the mountaintop is quenched. The winds have blown away smoke and left a frosty silence. Below, cloud deck reaches ghost-white to the rim of a night full of stars.

"You have lied to me throughout," says Wayfarer.

"I have not," denies Gaia. "The perceptions of this globe and its past through which I guided you were all true," as true as they were majestic.

"Until lately," retorts Wayfarer. "It has become clear that when Brannock returned, memories of his journey had been erased and falsehood written in. Had I not noticed abrupt frantic activity here and dispatched him to go see what it was—which you tried to dissuade me from—that man would have perished unknown."

"You presume to dispute about matters beyond your comprehension," says Gaia stiffly.

"Yes, your intellect is superior to mine." The admission does not ease the sternness: "But it will be your own kind among the stars to whom you must answer. I think you would be wise to begin with me."

"What do you intend?"

"First, to take the man Kalava back to his fellows. Shall I send Brannock with a flyer?"

"No, I will provide one, if this must be. But you do not, you cannot realize the harm in it."

"Tell me, if you are able."

"He will rejoin his crew as one anointed by their gods. And so will he come home, unless his vessel founders at sea."

"I will watch from afar."

"Lest my agents sink it?"

"After what else you have done, yes, I had best keep guard. Brannock made promises on my behalf which I will honor. Kalava shall have gold in abundance, and his chance to found his colony. What do you fear in this?"

"Chaos. The unforeseeable, the uncontrollable."

"Which you would loose anew."

"In my own way, in my own time." She broods for a while, perhaps a whole microsecond. "It was misfortune that Kalava made his voyage just when he did. I had hoped for a later, more civilized generation to start the settlement of Arctica. Still, I could have adapted my plan to the circumstances, kept myself hidden from him and his successors, had you not happened to be on the planet." Urgently: "It is not yet too late. If only by refraining from further action after you have restored him to his people, you can help me retrieve what would otherwise be lost."

"If I should."

"My dream is not evil."

"That is not for me to say. But I can say that it is, it has always been, merciless."

"Because reality is."

"The reality that you created for yourself, within yourself, need not have been so. But what Christian revealed to me—Yes, you glossed it over. These, you said," almost tearfully, if a quasi-god can weep, "are your children, born in your mind out of all the human souls that are in you. Their existence would be empty were they not left free of will, to make their own mistakes and find their own ways to happiness."

"Meanwhile, by observing them, I have learned much that was never known before, about what went into the making of us."

"I could have believed that. I could have believed that your interferences and your ultimate annihilations of history after history were acts of pity as well as science. You claimed they could be restarted if ever you determined what conditions would better them. It did seem strange that you set one line of them—or more?—not in Earth's goodly past but in the hard world of today. It seemed twice strange that you were reluctant to have this particular essay brought to light. But I assumed that you with your long experience and superior mentality, had reasons. Your attempt at secrecy might have been to avoid lengthy justifications to your kindred. I did not know, nor venture to judge. I would have left that to them.

"But then Kalava arrived."

Another mind-silence falls. At last Gaia says, very softly through the night, "Yes. Again humans live in the material universe."

"How long has it been?" asks Wayfarer with the same quietness.

"I made the first of them about fifty thousand years ago. Robots in human guise raised them from infancy. After that they were free."

"And, no doubt, expanding across the planet in their Stone Age, they killed off those big game animals. Yes, human. But why did you do it?"

"That humankind might live once more." A sigh as of time itself blowing past. "This is what you and those whom you serve will never fully understand. Too few humans went into them; and those who did, they were those who wanted the stars. You," every other node in the galactic brain, "have not felt the love of Earth, the need and longing for the primordial mother, that was in these many and many who remained with me. I do."

*How genuine is it?* wonders Wayfarer. *How sane is she?* "Could you not be content with your emulations?" he asks.

"No. How possibly? I cannot make a whole cosmos for them. I can only make them, the flesh-and-blood them, for the cosmos. Let them live in it not as machines or as flickerings within a machine, but as humans."

"On a planet soon dead?"

"They will, they must forge survival for themselves. I do not compel them, I do not dominate them with my nearness or any knowledge of it. That would be to stunt their spirits, turn them into pet animals or worse. I simply give guidance, not often, in the form of divinities in whom they would believe anyway at this stage of their societies, and simply toward the end of bringing them to a stable, high-technology civilization that can save them from the sun."

"Using what you learn from your shadow folk to suggest what the proper course of history may be?"

"Yes. How else should I know? Humankind is a chaotic phenomenon. Its actions and their consequences cannot be computed from first principles. Only by experiment and observation can we learn something about the nature of the race."

"Experiments done with conscious beings, aware of their pain. Oh, I see why you have kept most of your doings secret."

"I am not ashamed," declares Gaia. "I am proud. I gave life back to the race that gave life to us. They will make their own survival, I say. It may be that when they are able, they will move to the outer reaches of the Solar System, or some of them somehow even to the stars. It may be they will shield Earth or damp the sun. It is for them to decide, them to do. Not us, do you hear me? Them."

"The others yonder may feel differently. Alarmed or horrified, they may act to put an end to this."

"Why?" Gaia demands. "What threat is it to them?"

"None, I suppose. But there is a moral issue. What you are after is a purely human renascence, is it not? The former race went up in the machines, not because it was forced but because it chose, because that was the way by which the spirit could live and grow forever. You do not want this to happen afresh. You want to perpetuate war, tyranny, superstition, misery, instincts in mortal combat with each other, the ancient ape, the ancient beast of prey."

"I want to perpetuate the lover, parent, child, adventurer, artist, poet, prophet. Another element in the universe. Have we machines in our self-sureness every answer, every dream, that can ever be?"

Wayfarer hesitates. "It is not for me to say, it is for your peers."

"But now perhaps you see why I have kept my secrets and why I have argued and, yes, fought in my fashion against the plans of the galactic brain. Someday my humans must discover its existence. I can hope that then they will be ready to come to terms with it. But let those mighty presences appear among them within the next several thousand years—let signs and wonders, the changing of the heavens and the world, be everywhere— what freedom will be left for my children, save to cower and give worship? Afterward, what destiny for them, save to be animals in a preserve, forbidden any ventures that might endanger them, until at last, at best, they too drain away into the machines?"

Wayfarer speaks more strongly than before. "Is it better, what they might make for themselves? I cannot say. I do not know. But neither, Gaia, do you. And . . . the fate of Christian and Laurinda causes me to wonder about it."

"You know," she says, "that *they* desired humanness."

"They could have it again."

Imagine a crowned head shaking. "No. I do not suppose any other node would create a world to house their mortality, would either care to or believe it was right."

"Then why not you, who have so many worlds in you?"

Gaia is not vindictive. A mind like hers is above that. But she says, "I cannot take them. After such knowledge as they have tasted of, how could they return to me?" And to make new copies, free of memories that would weigh their days down with despair, would be meaningless.

"Yet—there at the end, I felt what Christian felt."

"And I felt what Laurinda felt. But now they are at peace in us."

"Because they are no more. I, though, am haunted," the least, rebellious bit, for a penalty of total awareness is that nothing can be ignored or forgotten. "And it raises questions that I expect Alpha will want answered, if answered they can be."

After a time that may actually be measurable less by quantum shivers than by the stars, Wayfarer says: "Let us bring those two back."

"Now it is you who are pitiless," Gaia says.

"I think we must."

"So be it, then."

The minds conjoin. The data are summoned and ordered. A configuration is established.

It does not emulate a living world or living bodies. The minds have agreed that that would be too powerful an allurement and torment. The subjects of their inquiry need to think clearly; but because the thought is to concern their inmost selves, they are enabled to feel as fully as they did in life.

Imagine a hollow darkness, and in it two ghosts who glimmer slowly into existence until they stand confronted before they stumble toward a phantom embrace.

"Oh, beloved, beloved, is it you?" Laurinda cries.

"Do you remember?" Christian whispers.

"I never forgot, not quite, not even at the heights of oneness."

"Nor I, quite."

They are silent a while, although the darkness shakes with the beating of the hearts they once had.

"Again," Laurinda says. "Always."

"Can that be?" wonders Christian.

Through the void of death, they perceive one speaking: "Gaia, if you will give Laurinda over to me, I will take her home with Christian—home into Alpha."

And another asks: "Child, do you desire this? You can be of Earth and of the new humanity."

She will share in those worlds, inner and outer, only as a memory borne by the great being to whom she will have returned; but if she departs, she will not have them at all.

"Once I chose you, Mother," Laurinda answers.

Christian senses the struggle she is waging with herself and tells her, "Do whatever you most wish, my dearest."

She turns back to him. "I will be with you. Forever with you."

And that too will be only as a memory, like him; but

what they were will be together, as one, and will live on, unforgotten.

"Farewell, child," says Gaia.

"Welcome," says Wayfarer.

The darkness collapses. The ghosts dissolve into him. He stands on the mountaintop ready to bear them away, a part of everything he has gained for those whose avatar he is.

"When will you go?" Gaia asks him.

"Soon," he tells her: soon, home to his own oneness.

And she will abide, waiting for the judgment from the stars.